ONE AGAINST THE MOON

By
DONALD A. WOLLHEIM

I0541542

ARMCHAIR FICTION
PO Box 4369, Medford, Oregon 97504

*For more information about Armchair Books and products, visit our
website at…*

www.armchairfiction.com

Or email us at…

armchairfiction@yahoo.com

A STOWAWAY ON THE FIRST ROCKET TO THE MOON...

Trapped in an underground cavern of the moon, Robin Carew faced possible death—alone! Starvation was postponed only briefly. He had the two rabbits and a monkey that had accompanied him in the untested atomic rocket not designed for human passengers. Rescue was unlikely. No one had discovered him hidden within the rocket before the blast-off. He could rely only on himself.

From the moment this latter-day Robinson Crusoe discovers edible plants within the lightless cavern, hope of survival grows in him. An underground river leads him to other caverns, where he encounters weird creatures and another being—one who speaks in an incomprehensible language. Thus begins a series of remarkable adventures, climaxed by the arrival of a second rocket that brings both danger and good fortune.

ABOUT DONALD A. WOLLHEIM...

Born October 1, 1914, he lived in New York City all his life. At first a free-lance writer of stories and articles mainly for science-fiction magazines, he began his career as editor in 1940. Between 1947 and 1951 he was the editor at the pioneering paperback publisher Avon Books. In 1952, Mr. Wollheim was invited to launch Ace Books and held the position of editor of their paperback line for many years. During that time he spearheaded the Ace Doubles series, which consisted of pairs of books, usually by different authors, bound back-to-back with two "front" covers.

He called Professor Tolkien in 1964 and asked if he could publish Lord of the Rings as an Ace paperback. Tolkien said he would never allow his great work, to appear in 'so degenerate a form' as the paperback book. However, after some legal side-stepping he was eventually able to bring the Tolkien classics to publication in paperback form.

One of Wollheim's short stories, "Mimic," was made into the feature film of the same name, released in 1997. In addition to being a top-flight editor, Wollheim wrote many short stories and novels during his career. One of his most remembered novels was "Secret of the Ninth Planet," which was published by the John Winston publishing company in the early '50s. Donald Wollheim passed away on November 2, 1990 at the age of 76.

CHAPTER ONE
To Dream of Stars

THAT MORNING began like all the preceding mornings of the past two years with the tinny jangling of the little alarm clock on Robin Carew's bureau. Opening his black eyes, he struggled into a sitting position on the narrow bed, reached out his hand and turned off the alarm. He yawned, swung his feet to the floor, rubbed his eyes. It was half past seven again of another workday morning.

There was no inkling that this day would be any different from others. It was Monday again, which meant the start of the next five and a half days' stretch of work. Sunday had come and gone, now just a memory of a walk in the city's small park and sitting on a bench under the afternoon sun reading a library book on astronomy.

Well, there was no getting around it, Robin thought. The stars, the glory of the heavens—for him perhaps they would always be just a daydream of his idle hours, never to be more than a vision of the imagination, a thrill to be shared only by the printed words of other men's observations and doings.

He got up, yawned his entire five foot three, stared in the tarnished mirror over the worn bureau. He looked blankly at himself, then suddenly winked. Ah, he thought, while there's life there's hope—and besides, he had to get to work. He ran a brush through his tousled brown hair, took off his pajamas, and climbed into his work clothes. Grabbing his towel and his toothbrush, he opened the door and went out into the hall toward the washroom.

The facilities at the Y were always clean at least, and maybe in a few more months he would be promoted out of the apprentice class at the factory. Then he could afford to get a bigger room on the floor above with his own washstand and shower.

After he had returned and finished dressing, he glanced out the narrow window. He could just make out a slit of sky and spot the sidewalk below. It was a sunny day, he saw, and a warm one. Putting on his jacket, he left his cap behind and went out, locking the door of his little room behind him.

Not waiting for the creaky elevator, he skipped down the iron stairs to the lobby. Waving hello to a couple of his fellow boarders, he made his way over to the newsstand. There he paused to glance at the headlines, to scan the racks of magazines to see if there were any he might think of buying that he hadn't seen before. He didn't notice any. His eye, rapidly discarding the featured stories in the papers about the usual crimes and politics, was caught by a small heading:

ROCKET PROGRAM AHEAD OF SCHEDULE—
PROJECT CHIEF REPORTS TESTS ARE MANY
MONTHS ADVANCED!

Robin stopped, rapidly glanced over the story. He wished he had the time to read the whole story, but he knew he hadn't. Anyway, he could probably borrow a copy during lunch hour from one of the fellows. But it was stories like that which fascinated him.

As he went into the cafeteria at the Y and sat eating a quick breakfast, he thought about the story. He'd always been fascinated by rockets and the stars. Even when still a kid at the orphanage, he'd read everything he could get on the subject. He'd never stopped doing so. Now that he was out of the school, out on his own the past three years, he still had the bug.

The White Sands and Redstone rocket experiments were making headlines more and more. The first dozen little satellites had been thrilling reading—the discussions of the permanent artificial satellite program, now under way, was even more so, for it promised to be the beginning of the long-projected Space Platform, from which in turn would come the first real space flight.

Robin wished he knew more of the things that were going on. Somewhere out there in the West, on the deserts and sands of New Mexico a couple of thousand miles away, history was being made. Many of the fellows working there couldn't be much older than he.

But fate was a grim and arbitrary thing. For others, a college education could bring to a fine point the talent for mathematics and chemistry and physics that was needed for this work. For an orphan boy, however, the world reserved less glamorous and more immediately practical objectives. Oh, sure, he'd had a chance at a scholarship, but somehow he just hadn't made it. The manual training programs stressed at the State Home had just not allowed him the extra time to study for a scholarship. Even though his instructors had given him the chance, he simply hadn't been able to make it.

For him, the study of abstract science was to be a matter of home reading. He'd devoured all the books in the library on the stars. And he still dreamed, even while working in the carpentry shop of the factory here, of flying through space on wings of flame.

Perhaps, if he'd had a mother and father like most fellows, he'd have gone to college, might even now be on his way to help the rocket men conquer the universe. But his folks had died somewhere in the holocaust of war, back during the fall of Hitler's Germany, back when he was just a frightened and helpless kid of seven.

As he had agreed a thousand times since then, Robin reflected, as he spooned cereal to his mouth, he was lucky even so. For somehow the GI's had found a battered, dirty envelope sewn into his worn internment-camp jacket with identification that proved him the American-born son of American parents, who had been interned in the enemy country. But where his parents were...well, there had been some terrible bombing in those days. There was never any trace of the Carews. Robin had only a vague memory of his people, somewhere lost amid a nightmare of terror.

As most of the kids in the orphanage had, Robin dreamed of someday finding his folks, of finding them rich. But it was, as always, a dream. The American army had brought him home, had sought to trace his folks, and had failed. Well, Robin still was lucky. It was no shame to be a workingman in a democratic country.

Time was passing. Robin hastily gulped down the glass of milk he knew he needed for his daily labors, and, paying his check, dashed out. He caught the bus at the corner, crowding in with others on their way, and rode it for fifteen minutes out to the edge of town where the big plant stood.

He jumped off and headed for the main gates. He noticed a large crowd of men standing in front of them. Why were they standing, he thought, why didn't they go on in, punch their cards? He came up to then, saw them standing around talking uneasily, some milling around, holding their lunch pails idly in their hands. Robin pushed through to the main gate. He saw a knot of men staring at a sign tacked on the post. He got closer and read it.

It was a statement from the management. It seemed that the plant was closed for six weeks, due to a combination of circumstances. There was a shortage in the raw materials because of the heavy floods in the mining areas that spring, and so the management had decided to take advantage of that shortage to retool and recondition the works. Men in several departments would be called in during the next few days, the rest would be laid off temporarily. Another notice tacked below that stated that the company had arranged with the union for compensation during the period.

Robin stared at the notice numbly for a minute. He himself had not yet been admitted to the union, for he was only a learning apprentice. For him there would possibly be only a period of six barren, workless weeks. He wandered away from the gates, drifted around idly, listening to the groups of men talking.

Most of them seemed to be taking it calmly enough. Several of them were talking with growing enthusiasm of organizing a hunting-and-fishing trip upstate for the next week or so. One was talking of going home to visit the old folks back at the farm. Most of them seemed to be looking forward more or less to a period of loafing around at home with their families.

Suddenly Robin felt more alone than usual. For him, there was no family. Even at its best an orphanage has a certain coldness, a certain impersonal precision that can never make up for the warmth of family life. He had friends there, but surely by this time they, too, had left, having gone into business or into the armed forces.

The cold halls of the Y offered no particular relaxation. Even utilizing the city library to burrow deep into his favorite imaginative studies of science seemed a barren prospect for six whole weeks.

He wandered away from the men, walked along the great factory wall, hands in his pockets, strolling slowly away from the city, along the road to the open country, beyond the end of the bus lines. He thought about himself. He took stock of himself.

Nearly twenty now, he was a good mechanic, a pretty good carpenter, handy. He'd always be able to get a job somewhere in which he could work with his hands. He'd never thought too much though about the future. He would be taken sooner or later by the armed forces. They hadn't needed him and he hadn't thought about volunteering first. He was always a little sensitive about his height, for he was short for his age. This had probably operated subconsciously to keep him from joining up.

I could sign up now, he thought. This might be the time. Besides, he went on in his reasoning, if I volunteered I could pick my own branch of the service. I could pick the Air Force and maybe get to see some rockets and jets in action. I couldn't rate a pilot's commission because I'm no college man, but I bet I could qualify as a mechanic, get to work on the rocket planes. Why, maybe I could even manage to get sent to White Sands, work on the Space Platform and the Artificial Satellites. Maybe someday I'll be one of the guys who help tool up the first rocket to the moon!

He found himself growing excited at the thought. But, he reminded himself, my chances are slim of getting what I want. There are so many good guys in the Air Force, my own chance of being sent to one particular place is small, really small.

Somehow, he knew if he couldn't be around the rockets, he wouldn't be happy under discipline. He'd had enough barracks life in the orphanage, more didn't appeal to him without some special compensation—something like White Sands.

So—he had six weeks with nothing to do. He walked on, beyond the town now, alongside the highway, the morning sun shining down, the blue sky beaming overhead, and he began to feel himself swelling with energy, glowing with ambition.

Six weeks…six weeks. He was young, he had no ties. Maybe he could hitchhike to White Sands in time to look around, maybe spot a rocket go winging off into the sky, then hitchhike back in time for the factory's reopening.

The idea blazed into his mind, he felt his pulse beating uncontrollably. Maybe, maybe, his mind added to the picture, maybe you could get a job in White Sands, near the field. Maybe they hire civilian workers? Or—maybe if you enlist there they'll let you serve there?

Abruptly he turned around, started walking rapidly back to the city. He'd do it, he told himself excitedly. He'd do it. He'd go back to the Y now, today, collect what he needed, take the few dollars he'd saved up, and go.

His mind repeated a rhythm as he walked. Do it now, if you don't do it now, you'll never do it. This is your chance. Go. The West is calling. The rockets are calling. Make a break for yourself. Go!

He reached the end of the bus line, hopped on the bus, vibrated in tune to his racing thoughts all the way back.

But an hour and a half later, when he was standing in the bus terminal, the first flush of excitement had drained away. Now he felt a cold chill running through him. He had made the break, packed a few necessities, drew his small reserve of cash from the bank, paid his room rent six weeks in advance, and bought a ticket on the bus going westward.

He couldn't afford the entire trip to New Mexico, so he bought passage for a few hundred miles. After that he'd hike and thumb rides the rest of the way. He didn't want to resort to charity so he had kept enough funds to keep him in food and lodgings if necessary and maybe take him part way home again.

For a moment before boarding the bus, Robin hesitated. Was it after all but a daydream that he was pursuing? Was the cold reality to prove too indifferent to the hopes of just an ordinary young fellow? Would White Sands prove a disappointment? Was this a mistake he would regret?

For just a second he hesitated and then, shaking his head angrily as if to drive out such thoughts, he stepped aboard the bus, slung his lightly packed valise onto the rack over an empty seat, and sat down. He would refuse to give up his vision. He would see this through.

The horn honked, two or three more passengers swung aboard, the driver threw in the clutch, and the bus drove out of the terminal, along the long, dusty road west.

CHAPTER TWO
White Sands or Red?

FROM MISSOURI where the bus ride had ended, the time had passed with difficulty. There had been two hot days through Kansas, standing by lonely roadsides while cars whizzed by without stopping, the strong sun beating down over the flat green plains, the insects alive with the fever of the endless wheat. Robin had to keep heading south, south and west always, driving down when cars were going that way. Down through Oklahoma, thumbing his way, sometimes with an Eastern tourist on his way to California, sometimes with a tired rancher or oil worker on a short haul to his home or town, sometimes with a bored truck driver anxious to have someone to talk to on the long trip.

The closer he drew to his objective, the more excited he became. When the oil fields and gray lands of Oklahoma began to turn to the green flatness of the Texas Panhandle he grew silent, more intense. And finally, one morning when he sped out of Amarillo sharing the high front seat of a giant trailer truck bound for El Paso, he was almost speechless for miles and miles. Then, suddenly, as the road clicked across the invisible border of New Mexico, he began to talk. A sudden calm invaded his nerves. He talked with the driver about things back home, exchanged comments on the affairs in the news, his eyes taking stock of this land all the time.

It was barren—for vast stretches dry desert and flat rock with only sparse clumps of desert green—now and then a stretch of good grasslands where cattle could be seen grazing. In the distance, gaunt mountain chains rose and fell; and the air was getting clear and thin as the road gradually rose in altitude.

After a bite in Roswell, when he piled back into the truck, Robin knew he was on his last stretch. After the next stop, Alamogordo, he would reach his destination, Las Cruces. Mention of Alamogordo, though, set the driver talking about the atom bomb, for that had been the town that had first seen the birth of that eerie fire which seemed so destined to transform the world.

"Did you ever see one of those blasts?" asked Robin quietly.

"Yeah," said the driver slowly. "Guess you could say so. Didn't actually see the thing itself, but I seen the glare one morning while putting over in Alamogordo. Quite a sight. You know the blast was plenty far away too; they don't fire them things off anywhere near where they can hurt anybody. Wisht I'd get to see one of them rockets go up they're always firing off at White Sands too. But I guess you gotta be on the grounds for that, and they don't let visitors hang around."

"No visitors?" asked Robin, a little uneasily.

"Nope. That's all top-secret stuff out there. Now that they got those man-made satellite projects in operation, it's even more so. Maybe they let a few reporters in on special occasions, or some high brass with clearance from Washington, but nobody else can get in. Can't even get the GI's who are out there to talk much about it. You'll see a lot of them around Las

Cruces Saturday nights on furlough but they just don't discuss it."

"How far is White Sands from Las Cruces?" asked Robin.

"Oh, not too far, maybe thirty miles. The proving grounds are out on the desert though, part of the Holloman Air Development Center that is taking up a lot of this here Tularosa Basin these years. Without a pass, you can't even get in sight of it. But, heck, you wouldn't want to, I hope. Might get conked when one of those whacking big rockets come down. They're always shooting 'em up on tests, making them bigger and bigger. You can't tell me they always know where they're going to come down!"

They passed Alamogordo, drove an hour more through the stillness of the desert, and suddenly they were in Las Cruces. The truck drew to a halt, and Robin dropped off, his valise in his hand. The city didn't seem aware of its unique position on the map of world history.

Robin trudged along the main street until he found a small hotel within his means. He got a room, washed from the trip, brushed his clothes. He had not taken any pants to spare, having put on a strong pair of khaki work trousers, figuring correctly that they were more the thing for hitchhiking than his one good Sunday suit. By the time he went downstairs night had fallen.

He got a bite to eat, walked around the town a bit, went back and to bed. He was dog-tired from the long day's ride.

Next day he walked the town, looking it over, asking questions about how to get to White Sands. He found that the truck driver's advice had been right. There simply was no way a visitor could just go and watch. It was all top-secret stuff, barred to any but legitimate personnel.

He found an Air Force recruiting office, went in, and talked with the sergeant in charge. Robin had begun to dread the thought that in the end he might have to go back to his home city and back to work in the factory. He had so fixed his mind on the rockets, he couldn't bring himself to admit defeat now.

The Air Force man confirmed the usual information. Robin pressed him to say whether if he signed up for the service in Las Cruces he wouldn't stand a good chance of being assigned there. The sergeant laughed.

"Well, it's possible, but it might take a little doing. You get in the Air Force, let us train you for a good job, say you work to be a mechanic for jets and rockets, then maybe you might be assigned here. But there are lots of stations for men, and you might not. Still, if you were to work for it, say after a year in service, you might apply for a transfer to White Sands; it could be that you could get it. But there's no guarantee, none at all. If the force needs you more somewhere else, that'll have to be it. Why not sign up and try for it?"

But Robin shook his head. "Not yet. I want to see if maybe I can get a civilian job there first, or maybe just visit it once."

The sergeant nodded. "You can try. After that, come around and see me again." Robin nodded, and left.

He thought about that as he walked the streets. It might be a good alternative. It did offer at least a chance at the work he dreamed of, at being near the rockets.

Yet—to be so near *now* and be stopped. A year, even in the Air Force, still seemed a mighty long time to wait.

He found the civilian employment office for the White Sands Proving Grounds, but it was not only closed, it being Saturday afternoon, but there was a sign saying, *No Help Wanted*.

That night he began to notice men in Air Force dress blues, others in GI khaki, and even some in ordinary olive-drab fatigues appearing in the streets. He realized it was Saturday night and the streets were beginning to show the signs of life for the men's one night a week in town. Ranchers were driving in, their cars lining the curbs. Buses bearing the name of White Sands would come in, unload their pleasure-hungry men, and park somewhere or else go back. White-capped MP's were appearing at corners to augment the local police.

Nevertheless, there was mighty little disturbance. There weren't the noisy carryings-on that usually marked towns near army bases when soldiers had a night off. These were picked men, and they behaved themselves.

Robin was not a drinker and not a roisterer, yet that evening he wondered if he oughtn't to have been. For if he could have learned to hang around some of the livelier bars, he might have been able to strike up conversations with the men of White Sands. After a while, he did indeed enter one, sat nursing a lone beer while listening to the men.

But they did not talk business. They talked the talk that soldiers on leave talk everywhere. Their girlfriends, their pals, their latest jokes, gossip, but never a word about rockets, never a word about satellites, never a whisper about their work.

Robin drifted with the crowd in the streets for several hours, finally again found another corner in a dim tavern where he sat, by this time a little tired, a little confused, wondering whether he had not made a mistake in coming here at all. The whole day had been frustration and his spirits were at low ebb.

Two men in fatigue denims were seated near him, arguing. One was plainly far-gone under the influence of liquor. He was bleary-eyed, nodding and mumbling. The other, trying to hold him, shaking him, was actually almost as far-gone. He was mumbling something about getting up and going; they had to make the last truck to camp.

Finally the two got up, staggered to the men's room, and disappeared inside. Robin resumed his meditations, noting that the place was nearly empty now, that the streets were silent. Obviously time had run out for the men, and they were on their way back to camp. Suddenly it occurred to him that the two soldiers had failed to come out of the lavatory.

Robin slipped out of his seat, opened the door of the washroom, and went in. The two men were there, together on the floor, sound asleep.

Hastily Robin knelt down, shook them. "Wake up, you got to go back to camp!" he called. But he couldn't budge them. One mumbled something without opening his eyes, slumped back, and began to snore. The other didn't even respond that much.

For a moment Robin stood beside them, thinking that he ought to go and tell the proprietor. Then he heard a voice call loudly outside in the bar:

"Any of youse guys going back tonight better step on it! Bus's leaving in two minutes!"

An MP rounding up the stragglers, Robin thought. And in that moment, a sudden chill ran through him, a sudden wild thought leaped into his head. He stood transfixed for an instant. For an instant which seemed to last an eternity, an instant in which all his training, all his instincts and ambitions fought and struggled together in a mad hysteria. Here was an opportunity, here was a chance—yet a trickery, an illegality.

If he borrowed one of the unconscious men's jackets, borrowed his pass, he could ride back to White Sands that very night, and in the dark and confusion, who would know?

Nobody, he felt sure. The next day—well, he'd be surely found, arrested. But—in the meantime, for a blessed hour or so, he would see the rockets in their gaunt glory, in their towering eminencies, see an assault against the skies, watch the hissing blue flame ascend to the heavens, see a sight he would remember with joy the rest of his life.

What then if he spent some bad hours under arrest? What even if he went to jail? Actually what could they do to him? He was no spy, he was no saboteur. No matter bow exhaustive the investigation, it would prove nothing evil against him.

He remembered a sermon that had once been given at the orphanage. He remembered the minister dwelling on the opportunities of life. He remembered that which had sparked his imagination then, the minister's depiction of the various roads each man must choose. "There comes a time," the speaker had said, "in every man's life when various roads open out before him, each leading in a different direction. If, at that moment, he makes his choice, then his entire life may be forever set upon a channel, and the other possible lives will vanish."

Was not this then such a crossroads? Robin could go back, be a factory hand, be a contented mechanic or carpenter, marry, settle down, and live his life without ever seeing rockets. Or he could take the road that now, for a brief flicker, seemed open to him.

He bent down, removed the khaki work jacket the smaller of the two men was wearing, shrugged his own shoulders into it, felt in its pocket, pulled out a folded piece of paper, glanced at it. *Pass,* it read. *Seven hours. Red Sands Station.*

He shoved it into his pocket, pushed open the wash-room door, and walked rapidly to the street, his head down.

As he emerged onto the street, he was grabbed roughly by an MP. "Hurry, feller," the man said. "What station?"

"Red Sands," muttered Robin in a low voice, and was instantly whirled around bodily and given a push. "Up the street and around the corner. The second bus. Run!"

Robin broke into a run, dashed around the corner. In the darkened side street, three buses were warming up, the first already beginning to roll. Robin ran for the second, and just as it was pulling away from the curb, several hands reached out of the door, took hold of Robin's hands, and heaved him aboard.

He found a seat in the back of the crowded bus, kept his head down to avoid having anybody realize he was a stranger, and caught his breath.

The bus gathered speed, roared down the quiet side streets, and turned onto the highway beyond the town. Robin was on his way to the rockets, to the famous White Sands Proving Grounds...or was he? What was the Red Sands Station anyway? *Red* Sands? Why had he never heard of it?

CHAPTER THREE
Up the Space Ladder

THE BUS roared on through the night, its cargo of men now mainly silent, dozing as their vehicle jolted along. The moon, which was full, shed a pale glow over the desolate landscape through which the road ran straight as an arrow. The vehicle had departed from the main highway fairly soon after leaving town, and had gone along another leading out into the wastes which was the government reserve. Robin had caught a momentary glimpse of floodlighted signs warning casual motorists against the use of the road, warning that it was U.S. property.

The men in the bus talked little. Most of them tired, and some a little the worse for a night's revels, were sleeping. Two or three snored away, unmindful of the hard seats and the jolting along the road. Seated in the back, shoulder to shoulder with several others, Robin kept quiet, watching the scene through the open windows and seeing what could be seen of the terrain without making his observations too obvious.

Thus far the landscape was the familiar desert of New Mexico, desolate and arid flatland with which Robin had become familiar on the trip down. On the horizon he could see the humps of mountains, the peaks that bordered the vast proving grounds.

Near him, a couple of soldiers were conversing in low tones and Robin caught snatches of their conversation. At first it was mainly talk of what they had seen and done that night, their girlfriends, and so on. By and by they began to talk a bit about their work. Robin strained his ears.

"I was thinking of asking for a transfer back to White Sands," said one of the men slowly. "Some of that new fuel they're bringing in makes me real uneasy."

"Ahh," said the other, "you're just letting that extra security talk give you nerves. Sure, it's supposed to be atomic stuff, new, maybe even untested as far as I know, but, nuts, you can't get blown up any worse than you can handling that liquid oxygen and peroxide they got at White Sands. In fact, I understand that this stuff isn't half as tricky to pour as the old stuff."

"Yeah, I know. I seen some of it being poured yesterday into that new big fellow they're lining up for tomorrow. But the point is that even if it's easier to pour—none of that fizzing and spitting you get when you leak a drop or two—it's atomic. That's the thing, atomic. What would happen if a White Sands rocket blew...it'd be a big bang, sure enough, but it wouldn't blow the whole countryside to bits. But take this new stuff...whew...we'd all be one Bikini if it went off all at once."

The other soldier was silent a moment. "Well," he said finally, "could be. On the other hand, I heard them say that it is really not half as explosive as the old stuff. That loxygen they use in the original Vikings is really dangerous, will go off quick at any spark. But this new stuff, it won't actually go off until it's touched off after the rocket has gone up a few miles. It's actually hard to blast—and then I understand they ain't sure it'll work."

The other one nodded. "Uh uh, so they say, but you notice where they moved our outfit, didn't you? They don't want to blow the main fields out of existence by accident, just in case they might be a little wrong. So they invented this Red Sands layout. I don't even like the name."

The soldiers fell silent awhile. Robin turned these words over carefully. He had read nothing of any Red Sands operation, and he remembered nothing of any talk about atomic fuels. In fact he'd understood that the problem was still one they had failed to solve—though the idea was intriguing.

Chemical fuels, he knew, had definitely limited drive capacities. The most powerful chemical fuels possible even theoretically were those already in use, and were basically merely liquid oxygen and liquid hydrogen. And he knew that the main obstacle that always had to be faced by rocket engineers was the tremendous quantities and weights of the fuels to be burned in order to lift even a single pound of cargo.

Atomic power, if liberated, had on the other hand almost unlimited possibilities as fuel. A mere pound or so of atomically liberated material could probably drive a spaceship a million miles with a full payload too. But how to combine atomic explosions with controlled rocket fire? The problem had never been answered—at least not in the magazine and newspaper stories he had ever read.

He thought about it awhile. Then the bus honked its horn. Robin craned his neck, looked forward. He saw they were paralleling a high wire fence and coming to a lighted area. A large sign on a wide road entrance branching off caught his eye and he read the magic words, *White Sands.*

For a moment he thought the bus was going to enter as the driver slowed down. They came abreast of the gateway but the driver merely honked and waved and passed it by, Robin catching a glimpse of whitewashed barracks and low hangar-like structures beyond the gate. Then they roared on into the moonlit night, on toward the empty reaches of the desert where the mountains loomed dark in the horizon.

Where was Red Sands? How far? Robin speculated on it. He had evidently hit on something more than he'd reckoned. This was a development unknown to the public. This was something that must have combined the special nature of the Los Alamos atomic testing grounds with the rocket grounds. And it was obviously tucked far away from them all.

Suppose they caught him there, would he get off as lightly as he might at White Sands? Where atomics was concerned, secrecy was still enforced, despite the release of much information due to the installation of peaceful atomic plants in various parts of the world. But everyone knew that the world was still merely at the threshold of atomic glories and the nations were still anxiously vying with each other for leadership.

He supposed that perhaps he might be sent to jail. He might perhaps be confined to the Red Sands grounds until such time as what he was to learn had become public property. That might take years! Robin squirmed a little as he thought over this possibility. It didn't appeal to him. Yet, the die was cast and there was now little he could do about it.

He could, he thought, surrender now to the men in the bus. In that way, he'd be stopped from entering the forbidden area at all and might then merely get a bawling out and be released. But something in him absolutely rebelled at the thought. This far he had gone, this far he had moved toward the realization of a dream that had held him from childhood. He would go on, and if he were to pay the penalties for trespassing, he would at least see what he was paying for. Maybe, maybe, he would yet see a rocket go off.

What was it the soldier had said, "that big fellow…for tomorrow." Then Robin would be in time.

The bus roared on for what seemed at least another hour. Finally it approached another fenced-in area, slowed down, and came to a halt briefly before a guarded gateway. The men stirred in their seats, the sleepers were nudged awake, everyone started to squirm around. The driver exchanged a few words with the guards, the bus shifted gears, rolled slowly through the gate, and came to a stop. Stiffly the men began to climb out.

Robin waited until about half the men had preceded him, then, keeping his head low, followed. As the men jumped down from the bus, they stepped up to an MP standing by and showed him their passes. He examined each with a flashlight, took it, and waved the men on.

Robin's feet hit the ground. Carefully keeping close to the man in front of him, he dug for the pass he'd found in his borrowed jacket. Holding it out, he stepped up to the guard. The pass was seized, scrutinized, and with a tap of the hand, Robin was waved on.

The men were striding off in the direction of a group of low, long buildings of the standard army barracks type. Robin took the same general direction, casting his eyes about trying to estimate where he was and what was around.

The moon was high and its light was strong in the clear desert air. A few dim bulbs showed on posts and one or two lights were flashed in the windows of the barracks. The men were heading directly for their beds—and Robin knew he had to head in the same direction if he did not wish to incur suspicion. It was a ticklish moment, for he did not dare do anything to arouse the suspicion that he was a stranger here.

It was a long walk across the parade grounds and he allowed as much space as possible to drag out between himself and the other men. He came closer to the dark barracks buildings, walked along toward a dark doorway through which another man had gone. Turning his head he saw no one near him who might be watching, and Robin stepped into the dark doorway, then quickly side-stepped, slipped around the side of the building, and walked silently down the dark space between the two adjoining barracks.

At the far end of the structures, remaining hidden in the shadow cast by the moon, he looked outward. He could see, stretching out beyond, the level ground of the desert. He could make out the structures of what looked like hangars and machine shops, and he could see a number of vehicles, trucks, and odd cranes parked around. Far away he caught a glimpse of something white. Was it a rocket?

He crouched in the shadow and waited. After a while he heard no more footsteps, he saw the last lights in the barracks flicker out and silence descend on the station. He glanced at his watch. It was about two in the morning.

Silently he moved out of the barracks' shadow, walked fast and softly to the shadow of the nearest truck. Reaching it, he paused, looked back. Nothing stirred. Proceeding in that fashion, Robin moved from shadow to shadow, keeping as little in the bright moonlight as he could. He reached a building, clearly a tool house. He walked along it, went on beyond, passed through the shadowed side of a long hangar, found a narrow roadway leading out to where the mysterious white object rested. He walked alongside it, half stooping, but feeling sure that no one had seen him. The Red Sands Station was silent.

The white object proved to be a good deal farther away than he'd thought. He knew that distances in the desert were very deceptive, felt himself growing tired. Why, this objective might be two or three miles away, he realized now, but only increased his pace as if in answer to his tiring frame. The cold, dry desert air was bracing, and nothing moved save the occasional scurry of some tiny rat or lizard.

What he had seen was indeed a rocket. It was at first a dot of white. Then it grew into a line of white like a snowy tree. As he neared it he realized its true dimensions. It was a tall giant rocket, as tall as an eight-story building, long and slim, towering in the desert like an obelisk left by some Aztec ruler. It was held by a framework of metal girders, like that of a newly completed

building whose outer skeleton had not yet been dis-
mantled. Near it stood a truck on high, thick wheels,
which bore a long, crane-like apparatus, resembling the
tentacles of some weird monster-insect. The rocket
stood with its four wide-flanged fins jutting out near the
base.

Robin stopped at its base and stared up. He studied
it, saw that it was apparently segmented, having lines of
cleavage that divided it into four parts, the one at the
pointed top being the shortest. This was a four-step
rocket, he recognized, and knew at that moment that
here also was a step beyond what the public knew.

He walked slowly around it, awed and silent. He
noticed now that there was a thin metal ladder running
up the standing framework. The crane in the truck was
for loading the top, he knew, but he could use this ladder
himself to climb up without trying to start the truck-
driven lift.

He reached the bottom rung of the skeleton ladder,
saw a sign attached to the framework. He looked at it,
saw a number, apparently the code designation of this
rocket. Glancing over it, the moonlight was not strong
enough to allow him to read the words. He looked at
the parked truck with the crane, walked over to it,
looked inside. He found a flashlight in the dashboard
compartment, took it. Lying over the seat was a pea
jacket. The air was cold and would become colder.
Robin borrowed it, shrugged into it. He saw a package
lying beneath it, lifted it. A couple of candy bars it was.
The driver must have had a sweet tooth. Robin stuffed
the candy into the pocket of the jacket, which had other
things in it as well.

He returned to the rocket, read the work sheet by his flashlight. Most of it was incomprehensible. He saw that the sheet referred only to the fueling. Steps two, three, and four were fueled. Step one, the big one at the base was still empty and he saw that it was marked for fueling by five that morning. Firing time, he noted, was set for six.

Robin glanced up. Here was a chance to examine the rocket completely. Glancing around again, he swung up the ladder, started the climb. The rocket's sides were welded metal, shiny and painted white. The various fuel sections were numbered in large black letters and the contents listed. He saw that the first and main fuel chamber occupied half of the length. The three upper sections, already loaded, he remembered, were marked in liters. The name of the fuel was meaningless to him. It must be, be thought, the atomic stuff the soldier had mentioned. This rocket could be a huge atomic bomb, he thought, chilled for a moment. But he continued climbing. At the very tip, he saw that two small, circular doors, like the escape hatches of submarines, were set flush in the side. One was closed, the upper and larger one was slightly ajar. He reached it, looked in. He flashed his light, peered around. It was a narrow, closet-like space, filling a section of the uppermost tip, just beneath the point of the top. It was padded and empty.

Robin looked out from his perch at the top of the ladder. He looked away across the desert to the distant buildings of the Red Sands Station. He started suddenly. Something was blinking in the distance. He strained his eyes. Two tiny white lights were moving toward him from far away. He heard the distant purr of a motor. A jeep was coming to the rocket from the Red Sands Station. Had they seen his flashlight? Were they coming to investigate?

He glanced desperately downward. The ground seemed so far away. He could never climb down the ladder in time to escape detection. The jeep was approaching swiftly. What could he do?

In a flash of inspiration, he saw the open port of the dark closet-space at the rocket's tip. He climbed into it, swinging out from the ladder, hovering over the abyss, swinging his legs into the dark, padded interior. He crammed himself into it, found he fitted it neatly with very little room to spare and, grasping the circular door, pulled it toward him. It swung shut on its oiled hinges, clicked tightly into place.

Robin crouched down, silent.

For a while there was dead silence. Robin wondered if he would be able to hear anything that went on outside, considering the padding of the little space. For once he was thankful for being so short. If he'd been a few inches taller, he'd have found his position very uncomfortable. It was cramped, but not unbearable.

He strained his ears, finally heard the vibrations of the jeep draw up to the base of the rocket and stop. He heard faint sounds, which must have been the muffled voices of the jeep's riders. He lay quietly, hoping he would not be discovered.

Outside, the jeep had come to a stop and the two men in the front seat stared around suspiciously. "I'd have sworn I saw a light for a moment out here," said the driver.

The other scratched his head, looked around, "I'd better get out and look around, just to be certain."

They both descended from the jeep. One went over and looked into the trucks and carriers, peering under them for possible hideaways. The other poked around the scaffolding at the base of the rocket. "This is the one they're firing off tomorrow, isn't it?" he asked when the other joined him after a moment.

"Yeah," answered his companion, "or rather this morning. In fact in only a few hours. They've only got to load the main fuel chambers and they're ready." He shined his flashlight on the operations chart, the same one that Robin had examined earlier. "I wonder how come they loaded the other three earlier. That's odd. I thought that stuff couldn't hang around too long."

"Don't you know," said the other, "this is that big top-secret experimental job they were working so fast on this week? Something to do with a new kind of fuel, fairly stable but loaded with radioactive elements. Some type of new compound which is supposed to add an atomic disintegration impetus when it goes off. Heard one of the engineers explain it as something like plutonium particles in suspension which get touched off atomically as they emerge in the rocket blast. They don't know for sure it will work."

The other looked up at the towering structure. "I guess that's how come they're sending it up first with the regular loxygen fuel—so if the whole thing goes bang at once, it'll be high enough up not to blow the rest of us to kingdom come." He walked around the base a bit, stopped, flashed his light down, and picked up something. It was a cardboard sign that had been lying on the ground. He looked at it a moment.

"Hey, this must have fallen from the cargo chamber," he said, showing his comrade the sign.

It read: *Instruments in place. Do not disturb.* He turned it over. On the back it read: *Ready for loading.*

"I better put this back where it fell from," he said, adding, "but which side is correct? Did you say they were firing it at six?"

At his companion's assent, he said, "Well, I guess maybe they must have loaded the cameras and radio equipment this afternoon. I'll go up, put this back, and check it."

The man started up the ladder, the same one that Robin had climbed a short while before. When he had arrived before the section where Robin lay hidden, he tried the circular door of that section. It was tightly shut. This signified to him that it was already loaded and without further thought he carefully attached the little sign reading *Do not disturb* to the door.

After a few more minutes' search, the two men climbed back in their jeep and drove back to the barracks-grounds.

Inside the rocket, Robin had been unable to hear what they had been saying. Their voices came to him heavily muffled and distorted and he could not recognize the words. He heard the man come up the scaffolding ladder and try the door. But it had been tight and it had not budged. Then he'd gone down and a little later Robin had heard the jeep drive away.

Robin lay there quietly on the soft padding and wondered how long he should stay in hiding. They might have left a man on guard or they might be keeping an eye on the rocket. If he came out right away, they might spot him. Better wait here a half-hour, he said to himself, and then tried to make himself more comfortable.

The day had been a long one and a tense one. He was more tired than he'd thought. The tiny, cramped cubbyhole in the nose of the rocket was pitch-dark, cushioned, and utterly quiet. Robin rested his eyes. Before he knew it, he was sound asleep. The air was close and became stale; Robin's slumber slowly became deep and drugged.

The sun rose at five and with it there arrived the men who would load and launch the rocket—several truckloads in fact, with a couple of tanks of fuel. The volatile liquids were readied for pouring into the tanks and chambers of the first and main firing section. The engineers arrived. They began to check the loads and the preparations.

"The instruments in place?" asked Major Bronck, who was in charge of this operation. His assistant, a civilian engineer, glanced up the ladder.

"According to the notice up there, they are. I don't remember seeing them installed myself, though. May have been done after we left yesterday."

"Who was in charge of them?" the major asked.

"Jackson, sir," the answer came, "but he hasn't been in camp today. Must have been left overnight in town."

The major frowned. "Well, I don't see the instruments around so I guess he loaded them all right. Sloppy way of doing things, though. I don't like it. In fact, I don't particularly like this whole job. It's too hasty, too irregular."

The other smiled, shrugged. "Can't help it. Big rush orders from Washington. They wouldn't even let us put this shot off till Monday. Had to get a fast test on this atomic fuel. I guess it's another of those things they think the Russians are up to."

"Ahh, that's always an excuse for rushing. But I still say haste makes waste. Well, anyway we've got our orders so off it goes this morning. Trackers on the job?"

"Sure, they're right on it. But we've still got to load the animals. This is going to be a high flier and the space-medicine people want in on it. Here's their stuff now."

A light truck rolled up and two men came out carrying a crate. One of the automatic rolling cranes lifted them all up to the nose of the rocket. There, just below the instrument compartment, they opened another port and installed their burden, shutting the compartment again and sealing it.

The major glanced at his watch, looked around. The main chamber was loaded, the tank had departed. At his order, the rolling scaffolding was swiftly detached and driven away. Now the rocket stood alone on its own fins, pointing skyward into the pink and orange dawn, its side a dazzling white, its nose a bright red, each section banded in green.

"How far do you think it will go?" the major asked his assistant.

"Anybody's guess," was the reply. "The fuel is untested and unpredictable. If this trick fuel fails to work, the whole thing will go up maybe six miles and then drop. If the atomic stuff turns into a bomb they'll hear the bang in Las Vegas. If it works as they expect, it might go up several hundred miles, maybe even more. It could make a better satellite rocket than the ones we've got up already. In fact that's what they're hoping. They think they may be able to make this the start of a real space-platform program—for once carrying a payload up worth the carrying. But who knows?"

The two climbed into a car and drove to where the concrete dugout was located. Entering it they nodded to the communications men and other engineers already gathered. The major took his place at the firing panel. He looked at his timer, waited a few minutes. Gradually the small talk ceased and a hush fell over the little guiding post. The major reached for the firing button.

Back in the rocket, Robin opened his eyes. The first thing he noticed when his head cleared from the grogginess of his deep sleep was a slight hissing noise somewhere below him. The air felt different in his little compartment. Somewhere a thin stream of oxygen was escaping into the chamber.

He twisted around, felt about with his hands, located it. There was a thin line of holes along the seam of the padding underneath him. Now he heard other noises. Below him, a faint chattering, a scolding, the sound of something scratching. He put his ear down near the hole from where the air was issuing and listened.

Yes, he thought to himself, animals. Somebody put some animals in the space just below me. Sounds like monkeys' chattering. Must be where the air is coming from.

He had a headache. Bad air in here, he thought, and realized that had it not been for the animals being placed below him, he might have suffocated in that space. It was then that he fully realized what had happened—that he'd fallen asleep.

The animals hadn't been there when he had first climbed in. So he must have slept for several hours at least. He squirmed around, reflecting on it, still not quite gathering his drugged wits together. That meant that the men must have arrived and started work on this rocket again.

He thought this over, and a great uneasiness came over him. He strove to remember something urgent, something he knew he had to bring back to mind. Something about five o'clock and six o'clock.

Loading time, launching time. Yes! They were firing this rocket at six! But what time was it now? How long had he slept? He looked at the luminous dial of his watch but was chagrined to find it had run down and he'd forgotten to wind it.

He glanced rapidly around his little space, wondering how he could find out whether it was already day. Several glimpses of light hit his eyes. He saw that in three or four places there were tiny glass openings no larger than would admit a thick wire. He tried to look through one, but all he could see was blue sky. It was morning then.

He strained his ears for outside noises, truck engines, men talking. But there was not a sound from outside. Only the faint squeakings of the animals below him. He twisted around again to face the little round door.

It was padded on the inside, it had no handle there, nothing to get a grip on. He scrabbled in the padding with his fingers, reached the rim, and tried to push. There was no give. It was airtight, automatically sealed.

He pushed against it, wondered what to do. He squirmed around against the padding, lay back with his head against the cushioning on the opposite side, his back resting on the floor padding, and put his feet against the side of the little door. Thus braced he was all set to shove the strength of his legs against the door in an effort to push it outward.

He was about to do so when the rocket went off.

CHAPTER FOUR
Riding the Atoms

SUDDENLY it felt as if a giant had placed his huge palm squarely on Robin's chest and was pushing him down. As he tried to exert pressure against the door, the counter pressure of the invisible hand increased. For an instant Robin was thunderstruck. Had he suddenly become weak? What was this?

His first emotion, that of amazement, changed in a split second to one of terror at his newly discovered weakness, and again from that to a feeling of stunned shock. There was no invisible hand! It was the rocket itself moving!

Without thinking, Robin struggled to rise, but his muscles could not obey him. In the first seconds the pressure on him was mild, he might have been able to move if he'd given some extra effort. But by the time his astonishment had worn off, the pressure had climbed beyond the limitations of the cramped space and his young muscles.

The rocket had started slowly as these great towering constructions do. The first blasts barely served to push it away from its launching guides. It seemed to tremble in every plate as if precariously perched upon the short, furious blast of yellow. Then the fiery tail lengthened as the tall, thin metal body rose slowly, lifted like a thin white pencil on the roaring cataract of burning gases

Now it was its own length from the ground, now pushing up faster, giving in split seconds the curious impression that it might topple over at any instant. But the steady rise gained in speed, the rocket pushed away from its burning tail ever faster, the fire turned from yellow to blue, and within a few more blinks of the eye it was hurtling into the sky, vanishing into a dot, and then was beyond sight.

To Robin it seemed again as if a giant hand were pressing down. He felt it spreading over his body, felt himself being pushed relentlessly by superior weight against the matting of the compartment floor. His head was thrust down as if by a giant forefinger of this invisible monster leaning over him. Now it seemed as if the giant, in maniacal malice, was leaning his weight on his hand, pressing on Robin, trying to shove him through the floor if possible.

He gasped for breath, could barely catch it against the growing pressure on his chest. His eyes sank into their sockets and he tried to close them but found the effort too much.

All about him there was a roaring sound, a humming and thrumming, and now began a thin, piercing whistling, which was the air outside rushing past. The whistle rapidly increased to an ear-splitting shriek, then vanished, leaving eddies of unheard auditory vibrations. Robin tried to close his mouth, which had been forced open by the prying finger of pressure. He felt as if in another moment he must cave in, be squashed flat. His brain reeled dizzily, then suddenly a merciful blackness fell over him and he knew no more.

At that very moment, though he could no longer sense it, there was a click, audible through the length of the vibrating column of metal, and the first section snapped off. Its great fuel tanks, so full of volatile gases an instant before, had emptied themselves in a fury of chemical combustion. The automatic releases had loosened the whole bottom half, the main fuel section, thrust it into space to fall and shatter upon the desert miles below. At that same split second, another series of relays touched off the second firing section.

The new firing tubes blasted into action. Of a design different from those that preceded it, of a design new to the world of man, the experimental jet burst forth. For an instant it seemed as if the pressure had vanished in the rocket, for a split second the rocket stopped accelerating as it waited for the new impact. Then like a blast of lightning newly released from a storm, a shot of energy flashed through the racing metal body. The giant hand came down on everything within it with a firmness and power not sensed before.

There was a blast now emerging from the tail of the flying rocket something like that of an atomic bomb, but not quite. It was not an explosion, but an atomic reaction. It was a rocket flare of an intensity and heat beyond all the potential of mere chemical reactions. It was atomic fire, chained and harnessed to the tail of a rocket.

The thin white pencil, reduced in length, raced on into the dark stratospheric sky.

Back at Red Sands there was intense excitement in the control dugout. Major Bronck was racing around, anxiously yelling into telephones, watching the checkers, trying to keep track of everything happening at once.

At first the ascent had been neat and according to routine. The crew in the dugout, the radar crew at the main camp, and the one co-operating with them from White Sands itself were checking all right. Then in an instant all three almost lost touch as their objective nearly swooped out of range. The trackers fought to get it back in focus, and one by one finally caught it again, farther and faster than they had planned for.

"It's running wild!" was the way one startled crew chief told the major. "Going up and out like crazy!"

The crew on the tracking telescopes racing around the desert were calling in their story. Visually they had lost it completely. They had gotten a nice set of telescopic photos of the first phase, then they had failed to adjust quickly enough to the unexpected second phase. Now they were sweeping the sky desperately hoping to pick it up again, but without success.

Major Bronck called for a check on the last and surest guide. Among the instruments loaded in the nose of the rocket was a radio tone-signal sender. As a last resort, they should be able to pick up that signal from the rocket itself, confirm the story they were getting from their radar men. But the men at the radio listening posts reported no sound. And when the major asked if they had had it in the first place, the men admitted that they had not. There had never been any buzz on the ether from the rocket at all!

At that moment, the main Red Sands camp got on the phone. A voice from the commander's office wanted to know why the instruments had not been loaded. It seems that the man responsible for them had just turned up at camp. Jackson had reported his jacket stolen, his pass along with it.

Therefore the instruments for whose installation he had been charged with were still reposing in the camp! There had been a series of bungles, the major thought, as he tried to explain the situation. Obviously the rocket had not been checked as it should have been. Obviously whoever had calculated the course and power of the new fuels had erred very considerably.

"But we've still got it on radar. Yes, sir. We'll hold it. We'll definitely see where it comes down, sir."

The major listened, white-faced, to the commander's angry spluttering. "Yes, I know, sir. Top-secret stuff. But even if it lands a thousand miles away, we'll know, we'll spot it. Even if it managed to assume a satellite orbit, we could keep track of it. It's still going straight up. It might make an orbit. If it did, there'd be no chance of it coming down intact for foreign examination. It would probably circle the Earth a few times in a wild ellipse and then burn up in the atmosphere. We won't lose it."

But lose it they did. The radars held it for two hours more, until finally it was beyond even the limits of their extended capacities. It was going up, up, and out, and even at the last there was no sign of it slowing down enough to form an orbit.

When they finally checked it off as permanently lost, they knew they had witnessed the dawn of a new era. This rocket had assumed and passed the escape velocity. It was headed out into the trackless bounds of outer space. It would never return to Earth.

There was even speculation that its last known course might intersect the Moon's orbit. Opinion in Washington, after all the reports were in, was divided on that. But, in spite of the bungling, the rocket had proved a valuable point. From that day onward, rocketry in the United States took a new tack.

Robin Carew was dreaming. He was falling down an elevator shaft, falling swiftly floor after floor. Looking down at him from the space at the top of the high shaft was a gigantic face, leering at him while stretching a giant arm down the shaft trying to reach him.

In his dream he had the curious mixed-up feeling of wishing the giant could catch him and stop his fall and at the same time being afraid that the giant might be successful and crush him in his huge fingers. He was falling, falling, and squirm as he might, the bottom of this terrible shaft was nowhere in sight.

Robin thrashed around, trying to grab a cable, trying to catch one of the innumerable doors as they rushed past. He banged his hand against one, grabbed tight, jerked.

His eyes snapped open, his mind struggled to gain a grasp of where he was. Nothing seemed to make sense. It was dark and he was bumping around in a tiny, tight space. Yet somehow he couldn't get his feet down, he still was falling. Suddenly he felt dizzy and then became aware of the aches all over his body.

He stopped thrashing, let himself rest. He bumped against the tight side again, took the opportunity to stretch his body out straight and found he could not. He was touching both sides of the narrow space.

His eyes found the space not entirely dark. A faint trace of light showed from a couple of spots somewhere in the dark enclosure. He realized where he was. He remembered now the take-off, the pressure. Why, he thought with a shock, the rocket went off. And I'm in it! We must be falling back to the sands now. In a few minutes we'll crash and that will be the end.

He waited awhile, expecting to be snuffed out at any instant. But there was nothing. Just silence. And now a faint rustling sound where something was stirring and squeaking below him. The animals, he thought, are alive in the space below me.

Then it occurred to him that he was not falling back, but perhaps falling away. His mind, which had been numbed from the pain and pressure, began to reassemble what he knew about rockets. And consciously the thought formed—the sensation of free fall is the same as the sensation of weightlessness found in space rockets. He thought he was falling, but was it not just as likely that instead he was simply beyond gravity?

He felt himself over for broken spots, but somehow miraculously he had not been damaged. His eyes burned and he supposed they were bloodshot. A smear of stickiness around his face convinced him he'd suffered a nosebleed. But otherwise he was sound. He patted the jacket he wore and his hand encountered the cylindrical hardness of the flashlight he'd borrowed from the supply truck. He took it out, snapped it on.

The little padded compartment was the same, the door still tightly wedged. He turned the light carefully around it, saw that the faint break in the total darkness before had come from two tiny openings—glass insets.

Probably, he thought, the openings for the instruments, possibly the lens spots for cameras.

He switched off his flashlight, put an eye to an opening. The spot of glass was thick but amazingly clear. He caught a glimpse of blue-black sky and a jagged line of misty gray and white, beneath which stretched the edge of a great brown-and-green bowl. He stared at it in puzzlement, watching it as it swung slowly away.

He realized that the rocket had developed a slow spin, that his viewing spot would gradually circle the region around him. And he realized that the great brownish bowl was the Earth.

From the darkness of the sky he realized that he must already be high in the stratosphere, possibly well beyond it. From the curvature of the horizon, he must be far up, several hundred miles, he guessed. And he could see that the curvature was increasing as he watched. The rocket was still traveling upward, traveling at an immense rate of speed. Its last rockets had blasted away and had left it with a heritage of unparalleled speed.

Robin screwed up his eyes again, mentally calculated. He revised his estimate of his height, doubled it, redoubled it. Why, he might be a thousand miles up, two thousand, perhaps many times that! How fast was he traveling?

He didn't know. He couldn't tell. He remembered the talk about atomic fuels he had overheard. Could it be that the inventors had miscalculated? Could it be that he was already in outer space, heading for the void, never to return to Earth?

He screwed his eye again to the outlet. In the short time since he'd first looked the sky had darkened. It was black, jet-black, and the stars were fiery points of white. The Earth now seemed like a ball, a vast ball whose fringes glowed with the pale mistiness of a sunlit blanket of air. But where he was there was no air. He was beyond any atmosphere. No whistling of atmospheric friction was present in the length of the silent rocket.

And then a blinding white glow poked a piercing beam through the tiny eyespot. It was the sun, unshielded, brilliant. In a moment the tiny ray vanished as the rocket continued its slow turning, but Robin in that instant had come to realize what had happened.

He was in outer space, beyond Earth, never to return. He was the first man to reach that untracked void that bounded on all the stars and suns of a universe. He was the first—but who would ever know? Who could ever hear of him, whose helpless body, imprisoned in its shining airtight shell, now seemed doomed to float unsuspected forever on the cosmic tides of inter-planetary space?

CHAPTER FIVE
Fall Without End

FOR A MOMENT Robin felt dizzy again, and the falling sensation wracked him. It was the weightlessness, he knew. The sensation of being without weight was the same as that of being in free fall. And he was operating beyond the effects of gravity. Somehow the atomic rocket fuels had been far greater or far more effective than the inventors had calculated. He knew that they had never intended this rocket to be shot beyond Earth's grip—for if they had, they would not have loaded it with the test animals and they would not have placed a parachute-release arrangement in the nose.

However, it now occurred to him he might be wrong about this. He had seen the reference to the parachute on the loading chart, and he now remembered lettering indicating parachute on the body of the rocket just above the little entryway to the topmost cargo compartment. Still, perhaps there was no parachute there.

He squirmed around again, trying to get used to the nauseating sensation of free fall. He felt as if he had to exert conscious effort to keep his stomach from turning inside out. He felt an impulse to scream, to thrash his hands, and he had to remind himself that it was an illusion.

For a while he just rested, floating in the little space, bumping steadily against one wall or another, with barely inches to spare. The tiny burning sunbeam pierced through again and vanished. Robin looked through the peephole.

It was the dead black of outer space now, a black beyond conception, black with nothing in it to reflect. And against it an inconceivable array of brilliant points of light—the stars in numbers beyond any seen through the blanket of atmosphere. White, with some yellows and reds, and a few bluish ones here and there. The Earth moved again into sight and it was distinctly smaller—though still an impressively vast bowl—but beginning distinctly to resemble a monstrous globe in bas-relief, breathtakingly impressive with its living face, its shifting misty veil of air and water vapor.

Robin became aware that he was thirsty. Yes, and hungry too. He took stock of his situation. He felt through his pockets, came up with one of the candy bars he had taken. He hefted it thoughtfully. Should he eat it now or save it?

That raised the question he had been unconsciously avoiding. Save it for what?

If he was indeed heading for the boundless regions of space, then he was a doomed man. If he ate now, it would mean that starvation would come sooner. If he delayed, doled it to himself in small bits, it could only prolong the agony awhile, but would not the result still be the same?

There was the chance, the odd chance that the rocket somehow might yet return to Earth. It might describe a circle, an arc, finally begin to fall back. If it did so, the parachute would operate and perhaps land Robin in safety.

Somehow it didn't seem likely to Robin, yet that chance existed. If so, it would have to return to Earth before a full starvation period could result in death. Robin had read somewhere that one could go without food for as much as thirty days, but without water for not more than seven or eight. If the rocket were describing an arc or a parabola, then it would surely start its return within less than that week's leeway.

With this in mind, Robin unwrapped the candy bar and ate it. The second one he would save as long as possible. But what about water?

The squeaking of the test animals broke in on his thoughts. Surely they must have been supplied with some sort of food for their flight? Robin switched himself around to face the floor and began to dig at the padding there. He managed to loosen it, pull it to one side, revealing the floor of the compartment. As he had hoped, it was not a metal plate. His own chamber, the one for the instruments, was not a section in itself but only part of a section paneled off by braced plasterboard. And what was more there were already holes drilled through it so that the air in both sections would be equalized.

This answered another question Robin had been trying to avoid. How was it the air was remaining fresh now, though it had gone stale while he was hiding? Apparently there was a small supply of oxygen operating automatically in the animal section that seeped through into the upper compartment too. Evidently once the rocket went into flight this started to work and would continue for the originally calculated period.

Robin dug his fingers into the openings and pulled. Gradually the plasterboard bent away and opened a space into the section below. He looked down, using his flashlight.

There were two cages below, well padded. In one, two little brown monkeys clung together floating just above the floor and looking terrified. They chattered when they saw him, but remained tightly locked in each other's arms. In the other, four small rabbits were placidly nibbling bits of lettuce, although one rabbit was upside down, another sideways on the side of the cage.

There were a couple of small boxes set in each cage, and Robin could see that they dispensed food and water to the animals at presumably regular intervals. Robin reached down next to the monkeys' cage and started to work loose the small water holder there. He found it slid out of place once he turned the holding bolt. As he drew the little flask upward, one of the monkeys made an effort to nip his finger, but he withdrew it in time.

The water flask drawn up into Robin's compartment made him feel better. This would make his stay a little more comfortable for a while. He felt sorry for the monkeys, who might go thirsty now, but he had a suspicion that the two little beasts were probably too hysterically frightened to eat or drink anyway. Robin wet his throat a little.

He looked back down, reached out, and investigated the food compartment. Sure enough, there were several bananas in the monkeys' food container. They would do also.

He glanced around the space below again. There were the oxygen tanks, set up with a timer, one gently hissing away. There also was a small heating unit with a thermostat that evidently kept the temperature in the animal division at a level—and almost certainly was doing the same for the whole section.

Robin grimaced to himself as he worked the padding back into place on the floor. He might manage to be quite comfortable for a while longer—a day or so more. While there's life, there's hope, he said to himself. Better check the parachute question, too, while I'm at it.

He reversed himself in a neatly executed weightless somersault and making what had once been his roof the floor, worked the padding out there. But here he was thwarted, for he found the rounded metal side of the section's nose. If there were a parachute, it obviously occupied its own compartment at the very tip of the rocket's nose.

He looked out the peephole from his upside-down perch, stared musingly at the panoply of the stars. He wondered if he could recognize a planet should one swing across his narrow field of vision, decided that perhaps he might not be able to do so, so vast were the number of stars present. He looked again at Earth, noticing that it had visibly rotated on its axis. That meant that time had passed, a good deal of it. Mentally he tried to calculate just how much. He was looking at the Eastern Hemisphere now, or a corner of it. At least half a day, or maybe a day and a half, or more. How could he tell how long he had been asleep, how long unconscious?

He realized that he was tired, that his body still ached from the painful take-off. He closed his eyes, and without actually wanting to, fell asleep.

His sleeping body swung slowly to and fro in the tiny space, bumping gently from one side to the other. As he slept he dreamed of falling, dreamed of falling over huge endless cliffs, of dropping down strange chasms, of being carried by huge birds and suddenly being dropped.

His subconscious mind would never give up the insistent awareness that his body was falling. It was a certain thing that such would be the dreams of anyone in space flight. The built-in machinery of self-protection identifies a sense of loss of weight with the automatic warning of a fall. Ten thousand thousand generations of climb from primeval arboreal ancestry found the warning valid—no conscious knowledge otherwise would ever shut off this instinctive alarm.

He awoke again with a start and a convulsive grasp for a tree branch. But he shook off the sensation and rubbed his eyes. He took another sip from the water flask, reached into the compartment below and took one of the bananas. The monkeys were still in each other's arms, but now asleep. The rabbits were nosing the corners of their cage as if everything were perfectly normal.

He looked through his peephole and saw the Moon.

It was large, it was vast, it took up most of the view in his range. It looked as close as the Earth had looked before. He looked upon the stupendous moonscape with awe. It was the vision one strains to see through a telescope. He had often paid a dime to look at it through the six-inch telescope at the City Science Museum. This was the same vision, but bigger and clearer, so very, very clear.

He could see only a small section of the Moon, but that was impressive. A particularly rugged area of jagged mountains, huge craters, high walled and wide bottomed, with long rills and ridges running across the surfaces.

It shone white under the sun, with immensely black shadows breaking it where the sun failed to penetrate. Yet there were more than whites and grays and blacks here. He saw that without the atmosphere of Earth there were other more delicate shadings. The sides of some mountains had bluish and greenish tinges, and more than one crater bottom showed a distinct faint tinge of pale green, or in other spots yellowish blotches. And in one small spot he distinctly saw a mistiness of the surface, saw that a faint fuzziness barred the clear sight of the crater bottom.

He stared with wonder at the sight and the Moon slowly turned out of his vision as the rocket turned. He looked away, deep in thought.

He had read enough about the Moon in his astronomical readings. He knew the various theories, the latest conjectures. He knew that mistiness, evidences of clouding had been seen often by astronomers, but the sight was nevertheless rare. No two astronomers ever happened to be looking at the same place at the same time. It was always one man's word, and it was never possible to predict such a thing, nor to photograph it.

He knew that those men who made a special study of the Moon recognized these things and had come to accept them as evidence that what was once regarded as a dead world was not entirely dead. They had charted these color shifts in certain spots, one or two areas could be predicted well enough to occasionally be provable to others. Pickering had seen many such color changes, had even attributed it to some sort of fast-growing vegetation.

Robin remembered that it was now largely believed that the Moon had not quite ceased its volcanic internal action. He recalled that astronomers had begun to admit that the evidence of these bits of mist and the further evidence of actual mapped changes in the Lunar topography had proved that something was still warm and boiling within the crust of Old Luna.

Then it occurred to Robin that if the Moon were that close to him, he might really be falling upon it!

He peered out, saw again a section of Luna in view. It was close. Evidently the nose of the rocket had indeed been propelled far beyond Earth's atmosphere, beyond its gravitational grip. If the Moon had been elsewhere, perhaps the rocket nose would have swung about and eventually returned to fall upon the Earth, as Robin had originally surmised. But by chance his orbit, that of the rocket nose in free space, had cut too close to the body of the Moon. The rocket was dangerously near to being seized in the grip of the Moon's gravity and pulled down to it.

Robin mulled this thought over and realized that it was possibly the truth. He glued his eye to the peephole and tried to determine where he was.

After a while, he saw that the Moon was gradually increasing in size. The rocket nose was definitely approaching the Lunar sphere. Because the Earth no longer swung in to view, Robin also realized that the rocket nose must have reversed itself, must be heading moonward, must be falling to the Moon!

It would fall faster and faster now, as its trip through space was ending. It was held in the grip of a new world and would speed to its final destruction like a meteoric bullet. It would be another meteor blasting into the surface to flash instantly into powder!

CHAPTER SIX
Target: Luna

Now that Robin recognized the certainty that he would never return, that he was a doomed man, a curious sort of change came over him. Up to this time, he had been carefully suppressing his inner thoughts, comforting himself with the hope that the trip would somehow end up safely. Yet while his mind was dwelling on that thought to the exclusion of others, his nerves had been under tension. He had felt himself continually on the edge of breakdown, in proximity to screaming.

But Robin had been trained well. His life had never been a particularly easy one and the crying had almost certainly got out of his system during the days when as a little boy he had wandered through a war-torn land hungry aid homeless. Life in an orphanage, at best, lacks much of the careful comforts of parents' hands, and those who had come out of such upbringing learn strong self-control early, learn to hold their jumping nerves in check at moments of tension and crisis.

Now that the conscious realization that a crash into the Moon was inevitable had forced itself into acceptance, Robin felt a slipping away of this tension. The die had been cast, the doubt had been removed. He actually felt an easing of his mind, felt himself able to take cooler estimate of his situation.

He curled himself up in his narrow, closet-like space as comfortably as possible and thought the matter over. He was hungry again and still thirsty and this time he ate the second candy bar without saving any. At the rate of speed he was traveling, it could not be many hours more before he flashed to a sudden, fiery, meteoric death. He turned that thought over in his mind, while he drank some more water.

A meteoric end, he thought, to flash like a blazing firebolt, to crash with the violence of an explosion against the dry, dusty surface of the Moon. It might have been spectacular to observe, but he would never know. He wondered if it would be seen from the Earth.

Suddenly, like an automatic switch being thrown on an electronic relay, a memory shot into his thoughts. He was well-read in astronomy, particularly on the subject of the Moon, and the thought that struck him was this: *Astronomers did not see meteors crash into the Moon!* They just didn't! And Moon observation under powerful telescopes was most exact; if even fair-sized meteors hit the Moon with the same explosive impact that they hit Earth, they would be seen beyond question. Further, since the Moon was a companion of the Earth, and our home planet was bombarded with countless meteors daily, the Moon must be a target of a like number. Of course, the meteors that hit Earth were almost entirely burned up by atmospheric friction long before reaching the surface.

But the Moon apparently had no atmosphere…there should have been nothing to prevent them from constantly battering the face of the Moon in a continuous, heavy rain of iron and rock. Lunar meteors should be visible all the time. But they were not!

So...what would really happen when his rocket hit the Moon?

Robin was tingling with strange excitement. Facing death as he was, he knew that even at the moment of dying he would be rewarded with at least one secret of the universe now unknown to men. What was the secret? He wracked his brain trying to bring back to memory all that he had read on that problem.

And he brought back the memory that during the past few years a growing number of astronomers had begun to believe that the Moon was not entirely without an atmosphere. It wasn't believed to have much of one, but it had been pointed out that most meteors to hit Earth burn up at least thirty miles high. And the atmosphere at that height on Earth was very, very thin. So thin indeed that if the Moon had a belt of air only that dense, it might not be particularly detectable from Earth, might not make much difference from the surface—it was almost a vacuum so far as living matter would be concerned—but it would suffice to burn up meteors!

So it seemed likely that his rocket nose would be heated to incandescence by the tenuous Lunar atmosphere and burn to ash long before it touched the surface. It wasn't a comforting thought—he rather preferred the original conception of crashing.

Robin smiled grimly to himself. A dismal prospect, indeed. He had somehow cherished the hope that at least some wreckage of his rocket would be scattered about the surface, to be discovered some day by the explorers of the future, perhaps hundreds of years later.

They would speculate upon it, perhaps trace it and in that way know that one Robin Carew had, in death, been the first to reach the Moon.

But to burn up on high, even that faint honor would be denied him!

He looked again through the peephole. The Moon was close now, very close. He looked down upon a heaving and fearful view—a vast sea of glistening white, with streaks and patches of gray, and here and there great gaping clefts of black. Huge ringed craters, their saw-toothed mountain walls soaring into the sky—and craters upon craters, big ones and little ones, broken ones, craters breaking into the boundaries of others, little ones dotting the bottom of big ones, cracks and clefts shooting from their bases; a ring of jagged mountains running across the moonscape; areas of apparently flat plains.

The sun was directly overhead, for it was still full moon and the glare was great, the shadows that mark the setting or rising of a Lunar day not too obvious, stunted patches of jet blackness. But the Moon was not entirely whites and grays, for indeed it was gently tinted in spots with other colorations. He could see for himself that there were greenish tints in some flat spots, yellowish and purpling areas. And yes, there was even in one tiny patch in a crater floor a faint cloudy mass, a mere haziness that indicated some sort of gaseous mist.

Robin drank in the scene, the view of another world, that world which has dazzled the dreamers of Earth for thousands of years. These might be his last moments, but he could not be denied the saturation of his senses.

The rocket was fast heading down toward a point near the center. The Moon was spreading out, filling the view, and the rocket's slow rotation no longer brought anything into view but moonscape, a constant shifting view, with wonders upon wonders moving into his eye's scope.

Robin drew back a moment, rubbed his arms, scratched his legs. He felt himself tingling, wondered if it were his nerves. He felt itchy, hoped his nerves would not give way. He thought to himself, I may have only minutes now. I shall watch till the end. Then he heard a faint, faint noise.

From somewhere there was a humming. The merest shadow of a hum, and Robin listened to it, startled. The humming rose in pitch, it was no dream, and as he sat, mouth open, amazed, there was a thin, high-pitched screaming outside the rocket and he suddenly began to feel heat.

Robin had but a second in which to think to himself, There's an atmosphere and we're burning up, when there came a new sound. A sort of *bloop* from over his head, a snapping noise, and something seemed to grab the rocket and jerk it upside down violently.

Robin was tossed in a sharp somersault, banging against the original floor of his compartment in a jumble of arms and legs. He sat up and realized that he was sitting—not floating—but actually sitting *against gravity's pull!* He scrambled onto his knees, peeped through his peephole.

The sky was back in view, the Moon was below the falling ship and he could see the edge of a huge, circular orange mass above him, straining and pulling. It was the parachute from the nose of the rocket. It was the orange parachute designed to land the instrument nose and the test animals safely in the New Mexico desert. And it had been set to open automatically upon the pressure of air when falling.

There was an atmosphere around the Moon then…a thin, thin one, but the delicate detonator of the chute had functioned. The great hemispheric mass of delicate nylon had opened, had found a purchase, and was dragging the rocket back from a disastrous burnout.

Robin breathed a sigh of relief, strained his eyes to see the moonscape again. The rocket was still falling, mighty fast it seemed. He could see the moonscape rise out, expand to fill the view. The rocket was warm now, definitely still heating from the thin friction. It vibrated and whistled but it swung in no breeze. It was moving too fast. In that almost unnoticeable belt of tenuous air there would be no winds that could deflect it. The parachute was open, but the air was not thick enough to do more than slow it down too gradually for it to be saved.

It would, he realized, still crash into the surface with a deadly force. It would hit like a shell from a cannon, and the explorers of the far future would have their mysterious fragments of tooled metal to speculate on.

Below him Robin saw the jagged mountain peaks reaching up for him into the dark black sky. He scanned it, remembering his Moon books, remembering the cold photos taken by distant Terrestrial cameras and the careful diagrams and names given by men long dead. He was hitting near the center of the Moon, a little above it, and the crater whose walls were reaching up…why he could even name it. He grinned wryly. It would be

Theophilus, and it seemed he would miss it, hit somewhere near it in a bay of the so-called Sea of Tranquility.

Rushing up toward him, Theophilus was no peaceful Greek ancient. It was a barren, toothed, rocky edge, miles up, without the snow that makes our mountains majestic, without a trace of the forests that conceal a mountain's jagged sides, without even the gentle weathering of lain and water.

And the Sea of Tranquility—a dark, wrinkled plain that looked as if it had gone through the agonies of torture ages past. The marks of almost-vanished volcanoes on it, pale circular rings like pocks of burst bubbles, rambling ridges, and ugly cracks, and here and there domes rising gray out of the surface, like the tops of giant bubbles working their way out of the dry and flaky crust.

Robin watched in dread fascination. He heard the whistling and shrieking of the rocket like a demon in torment. He himself was burning and itching as he was being baked, although he felt no fever. The rocket was warm but getting no warmer. The topmost peak of Theophilus was rushing up into his sky like a fast growing stone geyser.

He watched it shoot up, saw it grow, saw the ground become clearer and clearer, each ghastly detail spreading out, assuming three-dimension reality. Now the peak was on a level with his eyes, now it was beyond him, and he was in the last few seconds of his fall.

The rocket seemed to be slowing slightly. The atmosphere was possibly getting a trifle thicker at the surface, enough to prolong the agony a minute or two or three longer. Above him the parachute strained and twisted. But still the rocket was falling too fast. It rushed down, straining to complete its act of affinity with a new gravity, as if tired of its brief period of interplanetary freedom, and anxious to pledge allegiance to a new gravitational master.

Below, the moonscape was coming up fast. Robin could see well enough to begin to speculate where exactly he would hit. There was a small circle that must have been a crater scar. There were several dark lines that might be a network of cracks. And there was a dome.

He remembered those domes. They had been quite a recent discovery too. Not easily seen until latter-day instruments showed the surface of the Moon dotted with these odd bumps. Their nature was still a mystery.

It looked as if Robin would find out the hard way what their construction was. For now he was clearly heading directly for the center of the one below him. A bubble-top pushing out from the plain, hard and shiny like lava, glistening in the sun against the gray and dusty surface of the plain around it.

Theophilus's wall was already on the horizon, high and towering. And now Robin realized how terribly fast the rocket was still falling. The mountain was a measuring stick and it was fearful.

There was a moment of dreadful suspense as the rocket raced to a bull's eye on the upthrust center of the dome. The rounded surface rushed up.

Robin flattened himself against the padding, clutched his head in his hands, and stiffened himself. The rocket hummed against the thin air, it vibrated against the parachute, there was a terrible split second of shock when the bullet-shaped structure of the rocket's cargo nose made its contact with its Lunar target, and then a clap of sound in Robin's ear like a blockbuster going off.

CHAPTER SEVEN
The Honeycomb Place

ROBIN had no time to wonder why he had not been instantly killed by the crash, because the explosion on hitting the surface of the dome was followed instantly by a tremendous roaring sound that surrounded the entire rocket nose. This was in turn accompanied by a powerful pressure on the rocket, which threw Robin against the nose-end cushioning and held him there.

The pressure was not steady, changing as the roaring itself changed, with sudden bursts of sound, convulsive shoves, and changes in pitch. The rocket was being slowed by a terrific outward burst of gases, gases that must have been imprisoned in a huge volcanic bubble whose outermost surface was the dome, so mysterious to Terrestrial observers. By bursting through the thin lava shell, Robin's rocket had released these pent-up gases and was boring its way down on its still rapid momentum against the pressure of this column of gas.

Robin did not know this at the time, though he figured it out later. At the time, he had all he could do to keep himself from being battered black-and-blue by the jolting rocket. He kept his head clutched tightly in his arms, rode with the bumps and roars, and tried to keep his breath from being knocked out of his lungs.

There was another violent shock and crack and again the rocket bounced to a new flow of gases. It had slammed through one huge bubble, breaking through the bottom shell only to burst into a lower pocket of gas. The roaring subsided to a lower pitch as the new gases did not find the near-vacuum of the surface that the first gas bubble had opened upon. The rocket fell steadily, bursting through a third, and then a fourth such bubble. It was clear that the surface of the Moon, at least in that area, was a mass of congealed gas pockets, a honeycomb of thin-walled lava bubbles, perhaps quite deep.

The rocket was almost entirely devoid of its original space momentum by the time it hit the bottom of the last bubble, snapped the thin crust, and fell through it. This time there was a sudden hissing around the battered nose and a warmth began to flow through the body of the rocket. It was enveloped in a belt of hot steam through which it fell several hundred feet and then hit something with a loud splashing noise. The sound vanished as the rocket sank deep into the new substance, came to a halt, and bobbed back upward.

Robin had gotten hold of himself after the third bubble and was hanging on, mentally trying to estimate what had happened. This last sound had been familiar. It must have been water, and the bobbing back of the rocket to the surface confirmed his views. He felt the rocket bounce a couple of times and then subside to a gentle rocking and rolling.

Robin held on for a moment, getting his balance. In some ways the new motion was more disturbing than all that had gone before—the cylindrical body of the rocket, with its blunt end and its rounded nose, was twisting and turning as only can be done by a bottle tossed in a flowing stream. Robin tried to get hold of himself, orient himself to the odd seasick motion, then managed to work his way to the peephole.

He could see nothing. Whatever was outside was without light. But it sounded like water lapping against the sides, it felt like water's forces, and the rocket seemed definitely to be afloat. Robin used his flashlight, tried to direct its beam through the tiny camera outlet. After a little manipulation he succeeded in getting some reflection from outside.

It was water, and the rocket seemed to be floating rapidly along on some sort of dark subterraneous tide. Robin sat back, puzzled. Water—under the Moon?

He held on, still feeling a little dizzy, feeling dirty and itchy, but suddenly beneath it all a little thrilled and pleased. He had survived the crash by some miracle—he was on the Moon and alive! What next?

Next was quick to come. There was a sudden dip in the current and the rocket tilted forward as it shot down a spillway, down a violent decline on a raging torrent, sliding down an unseen waterfall for a surprisingly long time, leveling out at a fast clip, sliding down new tunnels through which the water raced, hitting the side of sharp turns with occasional glancing blows, down more dips and falls, spinning violently around in unseen whirlpools, and finally racing out on a fast stream to gradually slow down and finally come to rest, gently bobbing.

Robin had been knocked around during this breathless ride and only gradually did he realize it was over. Warily he raised his head from where he was sprawled in his tiny closet-compartment and waited. But the gentle bobbing continued.

He put his eye to the peephole and looked. There was a glow outside, a grayish, pale glow, but he could see that the nose of the rocket was somehow grounded on something dry while the tail was still in the water rocking to the current.

He considered his next course of action for a few seconds. It seemed as if he had a chance to escape from his vehicle at last. But escape to what?

Was there air outside, wherever it was that he found himself? If there were air, was it enough to sustain him? Might it not be poisonous or utterly lacking in oxygen?

Well, Robin thought to himself, there isn't really any choice. If I stay here, I'll starve to death or suffocate. If I go out, I may die even sooner. But now or later, if it has to be, it won't make any difference. Whatever the odds in favor of my being able to breathe here, I've got to take them.

He twisted around, found the circular port through which he had originally entered the rocket. He worked at it with his fingers, realizing that it might be quite difficult to open. He worked away the padding that lined the interior, found that it had an arrangement that had automatically sealed it when closed. There was no handle on the inside, for it had never been planned to be opened from that side. However, there were several screws over a small plate, and Robin set to work to unscrew them. He had a Boy Scout knife in his pants pocket—the kind with several blades—and with the back of the biggest blade he worked out the screws.

The panel off, he saw how the sealed gimbals worked, clicked them open and pushed open the door. It held tight for a moment, then popped open. There was a sudden drop in the pressure, Robin's ears popped, and he gasped for breath.

The air outside was lower in pressure than that inside the cargo nose of the rocket, which had been sealed at Earth level. But it was air and it was breathable. Robin drew in several deep lungfuls, savoring it.

It was oddly exhilarating, as if highly charged with oxygen. At the same time there was a smell of mold and dampness and a definite taste of sulfur and phosphorus like that just after a kitchen match has been lighted. Even so, the air was breathable.

Robin worked his head and shoulders through the narrow opening, slid forward and landed on hands and knees on the rocky surface. He got to his feet, looked around.

He was standing on the bank of a rushing stream of water, which was pouring out of a large gap in the side of a cliff. The cliff ran straight up, gently curving to form part of the ceiling several hundred feet overhead. The extent of this ceiling was impossible to determine— it was dark and obscure—but it seemed to Robin almost at once that he was in some sort of gigantic enclosed space—a vast cavern beneath the surface of the Moon, probably several miles beneath it.

The water coming from the underground falls rushed out to form a wide, shallow river, which flowed along one side of the cavern and widened out to a few hundred feet clear across to the farther wall. On Robin's side the floor of the cavern rose in a slow slope until it reached its wall perhaps three hundred feet away. Robin could not estimate the length of the cavern. Looking along the river bank, the cave seemed to become veiled in a general mistiness and gathering darkness.

The light itself came from no definite source, but seemed to emanate from the rocky walls and ceiling, from the clayey ground, and from the general atmosphere. Robin supposed that the source was a natural phosphorescence, which he knew was not too uncommon even in Terrestrial caverns.

All around on the soil bordering the flowing water was a forest, a forest with the weirdest vegetation Robin had ever seen. Plants growing in clumps and clusters, plants whose large treelike stalks resembled a whitish--blue bamboo, and which burst into globular blue bulbs which seemed to serve as leaves. Among these tree-sized growths was a rich undergrowth of tight balls of varying yellow and green and purple, growing like thick, squat mushrooms. And everywhere else a thick, lush carpet of green, not grass-like but rather like some over-size moss.

In this forest there were no sounds of birds or animals, but only that of plants swaying in the river breeze, the rushing of the waters, and from somewhere distant in the unseen end of the cavern a strange, steady hissing sound.

The rocket, or what was left of it, lay wedged against a section of the bank, its nose up and its tail swaying in the current. Robin looked at it, amazed to find it so small. All that was left of the rocket was the cargo nose, which was the only part sent off after the last of the rocket sections had discharged their forces and been dropped off. The whole affair was not more than about ten feet long, from the battered, blunted red nose, from which several long, straggling orange cords hung—all that was left of the parachute and its attachments—down to the scraped and battered white cylinder that was the cargo compartment. The compartment ended in a flat plate which bore only a few wires that had once connected it with the break-away mechanism of the last of the atomic blasting chambers. This alone was the load of the eight-story tower of energy, which had been the Red Sands experimental rocket.

Robin, without further delay, bent down to the cylinder and began to haul and push it entirely out of the water to the dry ground. He knew he could not afford to risk its loss. To his surprise, moving the rocker head was an easy task. It was extremely light and he found himself possessed of tremendous strength, tired and bruised and sore as he was.

It was, he thought, as he pulled the rocket along, the Moon and its weak gravity. He would only weigh a sixth of his Earth weight here, so would the cargo head, yet he would have the muscles necessary for much more than that weight. He would literally be a superman here—if he could survive.

Survival, he knew, would be the question. He didn't know whether even now he might be inhaling poison from the strange, thin sublunar air. He didn't know what mysterious radioactive rays might be bathing him with their baleful influence. He didn't know whether any of t he vegetation in this cavern world would be edible.

Having brought the cargo cylinder to a safe spot many feet from the water, Robin looked for the door that would open the animal compartment. He found it, forced it open. Inside were the two cages. Gently he reached in, unscrewed them from their holdings, and lifted them out.

One of the monkeys was dead, probably killed by some of the jouncing the rocket had taken. The other, looking miserable, was clinging to the bars chattering. Robin looked at it, and the monkey looked back. The young man unlatched the cage, reached in, and took the little brown animal by the back of the neck. But the monkey made no effort to bite. Instead, it twisted around, grabbed Robin's arm, and hung tight.

When his grip was released, the monkey scurried up Robin's arm and clung to his shoulder, recognizing the need for companionship after its frightening experiences.

The rabbits had fared slightly better. One of them was dead, but the other three, while somewhat beaten around, were alive and sniffling their pink noses. Robin saw that there was very little food or water left for the animals.

Here then was the means to test the Moon's capacity to produce food and drink. First, however, Robin decided he would build a pen for the rabbits. If he were lucky, he could breed them and have at least one source of food suited to his system.

He went over to the nearest clump of ball-trees, looked them over, tested his strength on them. They broke easily and quickly when he grasped one by the trunk and pulled. He found that it could be splintered into shreds fairly rapidly and that inside the shell of the stalk was a mass of cottony matter.

He shredded a number of the stalks, and then staked them out in the ground to make a small fenced pen, tying the whole together with one of the long cords hanging from the parachute nose. Into this makeshift pen, he released all three of the rabbits. He filled up the cup from their cage with water from the river, then placed it in the pen. The rabbits eventually hopped over, sniffed, and drank. They seemed not to suffer from any ill effects.

Robin broke open one of the ball-like growths from the tree, found it contained a substance resembling a combination of melon and potato. He offered some of this to the rabbits and after an interval they ate it and seemed to like it.

The monkey was chattering away as Robin did this and suddenly scampered down and snatched a piece of the ball-food, stuffing it quickly into its mouth. Robin had not wanted to use the little creature for a test but the damage was done. However, the monkey seemed to enjoy it.

Robin sat down on the ground and watched. He felt tired, now realized just how tired he was, how sorely he ached from his experience. He felt warm and headachy now that the strain was over. He knew he still had things to do. He wanted to try to make a fire and cook the rabbit that had been killed. He was thirsty as well. He wanted to tie a cord to the monkey so that the animal would not run away into the unknown and possibly dangerous regions of the cavern. He wanted to find a safe place to sleep and hide should there be some sort of animal life around.

But he was growing terribly sleepy and feeling quite sick. He curled up, and before he could stop himself, he was asleep.

The rabbits nibbled on. The monkey sat on a ball in one of the strange trees and watched in silence. Far off, somewhere in the cavern, the mysterious hissing continued.

CHAPTER EIGHT
Robinson Crusoe Carew

WHEN Robin Carew opened his eyes, he knew he was a very sick man. He felt warm, sticky, and he hurt all over. He tried to sit up, but everything spun dizzily around him. His arms, legs, and body were burning intolerably and there was an itch throughout him that he could do nothing about. He lay back, trying to gain strength.

A little later he managed to crawl to the water's edge, fill the container he had used in the trip from Earth, drag himself back. For a period whose length he could not determine he lay helpless in fever and pain, arousing himself only long enough to drink to soothe his tortured body.

Finally, the fever broke. He sat up, feeling weak but with his mind clear at long last. He dragged himself to his feet, blessing the light gravity, aware that if he were back home his body would not have responded. He felt that he was gaunt, he knew he had been through a terrible siege, and he could only guess at the time he had lain there, tossing about on the strange Lunar ground, unprotected in the queer climate of this unknown cavern. It must, he felt, have been days—Earth days, of course—that his attack had lasted.

Later on he decided that he had suffered from a severe case of space burn. Having traveled through the emptiness of the void between the planets, the vessel had been nearly unprotected from the cosmic rays and the more penetrating of the sun's invisible rays. He considered himself lucky to have survived at all.

He desperately needed food now to rebuild his body.

He looked at the rabbit pen. The little animals were there and evidently prospering on the ball-food he had prepared for them before his sickness. It was almost all gone and he broke open and pared more at once. He wondered how long it would be before the animals bred—he knew that rabbits bred fast and abundantly, and hoped it would hold true on the Moon.

There was a sudden chattering in one of the strange trees and he looked up to see a little brown face peering at him. In a moment, the monkey leaped to the ground, then leaped in one tremendous jump to Robin's shoulder and perched there happy at finding companionship again. The monkey looked none the worse for its experience and evidently was getting along nicely on the Lunar vegetation. Thus encouraged, Robin fed himself, first carefully testing everything on the monkey, who objected to nothing.

But somehow the food was not entirely satisfying to the man, who felt that he needed more than that to recover his full energy. He looked again at the rabbits, looked also for the carcass of the dead one. But he found that part of it had rotted and part had been consumed. He looked closely and saw his first glimpse of a Lunar counterpart to animal life.

There were many tiny creatures, a half inch to an inch in length, looking at first like ants but on closer inspection appearing more like three-segmented worms, for they lacked legs and moved in an inchworm's fashion. Instead of antennae, each little worm-ant had on its front segment a single upstanding stalk ending in a little yellow ball. Robin touched one of these and it glowed momentarily. An organ of light, he thought, something like the ones carried by deep-sea fishes. The tiny things were eating the dead rabbit.

Robin went back and examined the three remaining rabbits. Two were males and the female was evidently heavy with young. Well, he could afford to dispense with one of the males, then, for he knew his body needed meat.

He put the rabbit back though, realizing that first he must make a fire and determine how to cook his meal. He searched his pockets. He was wearing the GI jacket he'd taken from the soldier in Las Cruces. As he had hoped, he dug up a pack of matches in one pocket. He turned it over in thought. When this pack was used up, how could he make fire?

He piled some trunks of dead tree stalks in a cleared spot; he lit them with one of his matches. They caught fire rapidly and soon he had a nice blaze going. He watched the smoke rise and saw that it drifted rapidly away in the same direction the current was flowing—-evidence of more caverns somewhere beyond.

He opened his scout knife, hesitated. He'd never cooked a rabbit before. In fact, he'd never had occasion to cook anything for himself. It was meat, he thought, and even if it were eaten raw—well, savages did, so he, too, could manage. He thought about boiling it in water, then realized that the light air pressure might allow water to boil without getting the necessary cooking effects.

The best method therefore was to fry it where he could observe the progress.

Steeling himself, he seized the rabbit, killed and skinned it, the latter a process, which he found thoroughly unpleasant. Cleaning it of its entrails, another unpleasant task, he cut the meat up into sizable chunks, skewered a couple of pieces on a metal rod which had been part of one of the cages from the rocket, and sat down to cook it over the open fire.

It turned out to be a longer job than he'd thought, and he burned the meat quite thoroughly in the process, but finally he made it edible and chewed it slowly. He needed salt, he realized, and wondered if he could find any. This would have priority when he began his explorations.

He hung the balance of the meat on a ball-tree with a piece of cord. He had seen no evidence of flying insects or creatures, and hoped thereby to be able to preserve the rest of the meat.

Thus fed, he sat down and began to map out his course. I must do things systematically, he told himself. I must keep track of time, set up a regular pattern of living, find a permanent base of operations. I shall have to explore this cavern and those beyond it, find all possible enemies and invent ways and means of defending myself. I shall have to breed my rabbits in quantity, find a way of using their pelts and fur. I shall have to determine a use for everything left from the rocket's material—metals and the like.

For, he continued telling himself, my one aim shall be to stay alive long enough to be found some day by exploring rockets from Earth. I am a Robinson Crusoe of a new world. Crusoe waited twenty-eight years for rescue, I must be as courageous. In his case, he had no evidence that any ship would ever bother to call on him. In my case I know that rockets are being made that will eventually lead to further Moon trips. I know that men are planning to come here. I must wait it out, even for twenty-eight years.

But it was not that simple and he knew it. But first things first, and the first task was to survive.

With the monkey scampering on ahead, he set out to walk to the cavern wall. He found it to be dark and glistening, a lava-like sheet resembling the bubble it was. Leaning against it and looking upward, he saw that it curved gradually up, and that indeed he was in a flaw within a very porous world. Like the inside of a Clark candy bar, he thought, with a wry smile.

Astronomers on Earth had always been puzzled by the lightness of the Moon. They had speculated on it as being mainly pumice. Lately there had been much speculation and opinion holding forth the theory that the Moon was porous, had these bubbles and air pockets all through it, that the Moon's water and atmosphere had all gone underground to be sealed off in these hollow spaces. He now knew they were right.

Most of these Moon bubbles, large enough to hold cities, must be entirely sealed off. But others were linked, sometimes broken into by quakes or the volcanic action, which was still going on in the depths of what had once been considered a dead world. This particular cavern was such a bubble.

Robin walked along the outer wall and saw a dark black spot in it, and then others. He came to them, found they were breaks in the surface, pocks caused by smaller bubbles. He looked into one that opened at the base. Using his flashlight, he could see that it was a small, almost entirely spherical cave. He found others pecking the walls of the cavern bubble.

This then was the ideal spot for a permanent home.

Not that he needed shielding from the elements, for obviously there were no elements here—no rain, snow, clouds, or weather oddities. Neither was there night or day.

Robin would move his possessions into this cave, simply to have them located and safe. Besides, there might be some larger form of life, some carnivores around—he could not tell. Better to be safe than sorry, he said to himself.

He acted at once, carrying the rocket nose and its stuff to the cave, transferring his rabbits and their pen to a spot just outside the cave door. He would need a bowl for water and, using his screwdriver blade, he finally managed to detach the curved rocket nose and found himself in possession of a deep bowl. He took this down to the water, filled it and carried it back to his cave.

Already he began to feel cheerier. Nothing like work, he thought, to take your mind off your other problems. Suddenly he realized he was tired.

How long had he been at this? He did not know. Now he realized that with no sunrise or sunset visible in his underground world, he could not tell time. He looked at his wrist watch, but it had stopped running, of course. He decided to take a nap; he lay down and fell asleep.

When he woke up, he set his watch at eight o'clock, decided to consider this the beginning of a day. He found the notebook he'd carried in his back pocket, opened it, and set up his new calendar. Using the date of the rocket's take-off, he allowed five days as a probable estimate of the time passed since. He had no means of knowing how long he had been ill, he suspected it had been longer, but decided to let it stand. After arriving at the date, he made the time eight in the morning, laid out the times he expected to eat, to work, to sleep. He would try to live according to a full Terrestrial day, checking the passage of time by his watch.

He then listed all the things he expected would have to be done, and decided to check them off as he completed them. Next he ate breakfast from the fruit of the ball-tree. He spent the rest of that morning trying to find a means of making fire. He had some bits of steel from the rocket, and he tried to strike sparks on everything that resembled rock. After a search, he found some fragments of rock near the water that gave off a spark. Whether these were flints or not, he did not care, so long as they worked for him.

With this discovery he knew he would be free from worry about the problem of matches. His next problem was to secure a weapon. This solved itself rather fast with a bow and arrow. A long, flexible metal tube from the rear connections of the rocket, bent to make a bow when tied with a string of nylon cord, made a satisfactory *twang* when pulled. He made arrows out of the fibers of the Moontree stalks, and practiced shooting.

The next few days followed the same pattern. Robin enlarged his area of exploration, finding several other kinds of Lunar vegetation and a number of other insect-worms. He found several that were quite large, one as large as a squirrel. It was an odd thing, humping itself along in little bounds—a creature of a dozen ball-like segments, two of which had toothed mouths, although only the ball in front had an eye, a lidless orb set in the center of this ball. But the creature was fringed with the light-rod organs as the tiny worm-ants had been.

Robin tried to cook part of this creature but the monkey refused to touch it and he found it entirely unpalatable. On the other hand, he found that when he removed the little yellow balls from the top of the light stalks on the creature, they remained glowing—even as do the abdomens of fireflies. He therefore diligently set about catching a number of these Moonrats, as he named them, and making a lantern for himself by filling a glass tube with the glow organs. This worked out quite nicely when he experimented in his dark cave-home, emitting a clear, though pale, yellow light.

His rabbit had a nice litter at last, and Robin carefully saw that they were kept well supplied with food and drink. He would eat no more meat until there were several dozen adults, all breeding. But he felt that now he was assured of a source of clothing when his own would give out. He knew that eventually he would have to dress himself entirely in the products of his own ingenuity. His Earth clothes could last no more than a few years. He had already devised for himself an experimental pair of sandals from the rinds of the ball-tree fruit and the stalks of the Moontrees. They would do, and he carefully removed his shoes and put them away. When he had heavy exploring to do, or if and when he might try to reach the surface, he would need his good heavy leather shoes. Until then, the makeshift sandals would do.

For he knew that someday he would have to reach the surface. If and when the first astronauts arrived, they would not go below. They would probably never suspect the presence of these unseen areas beneath the crust, possibly not for many dozens of years. It would be on the surface that Robin would have to go to find rescue. That was the greatest problem he would have to solve. Against that terrible trip, he would have to conserve and plan.

Meanwhile, he had a toehold on life here, if conditions within his sublunar cavern did not change. But they were changing…and not for the better.

CHAPTER NINE
From Stone Age to Iron Age

WHEN he woke up one morning Robin was vaguely aware of something different. He opened his eyes to the dark interior of his cave-home and lay there on his bed of padding from the cargo chamber. For a while he rested quietly in that pleasant half-sleep of awakening after a good rest. Unconsciously his hand moved down searching for a blanket, but of course there was none. He'd never needed one before.

He unconsciously groped again for the blanket, then opened his eyes wide and sat up. There was a slight chill in the air at that! Now he noticed the monkey, asleep, curled up tightly against his leg. That was odd because previously the little fellow had slept outside. What had brought him in?

Robin got up and Cheeky, as Robin had named his friend, woke up instantly and leaped to his shoulder. "What's the trouble, fellow?" asked Robin, patting him on the head. Then the young man left the cave and looked around. At first nothing seemed greatly changed. The temperature had dropped a few degrees, no doubt about it. Yet there was no special draft, no break in the bubble walls to account for it.

He looked at the plants and then realized that some of them were beginning to change color. A grayness was creeping in subtly. The balls of Moontree fruit, which had been his chief sustenance, were showing signs of wrinkling and had either already shriveled or were beginning to.

Robin glanced around sharply, looked into his notebook calendar. He calculated the days that had passed. When his rocket had crashed the Moon had been full. This meant it was high noon of a Lunar day on the surface above. But a Lunar day lasted about a Terrestrial month—twenty-eight days to be exact. When the sun was at its height, the temperature of the surface crust was to be measured as high as 240 degrees Fahrenheit. By sunset it might be down to 160 degrees, but immediately after sunset it would drop with great speed and shortly begin to go as low as a hundred below zero and continue to drop for yet another hundred degrees.

And Robin had perhaps been in his sublunar cavern for ten or maybe twelve days. The sun had set above, the Lunar night was there. Though the cavern was insulated by the best sort of insulation in the universe—a honeycomb of several miles between the surface and itself—a honeycomb in many cases consisting of sealed bubbles, some near vacuums—there was bound to be a gradual loss of the stored-up heat from the long Lunar day. It might take a while for this to become noticeable, especially in view of the obviously warm volcanic action from the unseen areas near the core of the Moon below, yet there it was.

So now Robin knew that the Lunar day did have a counterpart here, that there would be monthly seasons in his cavern and that he was facing a winter that might last ten days or more.

He looked around, pondering this. Could he survive? He had probably only a short time to work this out. Obviously he had to work fast and make good.

"Come, Cheeky," he said, "no time for foolishness. No daily swim in the river this morning. Harvest time is here."

He glanced at his rabbits, but they did not seem to mind the temperature drop. He went into the clumps of Moontrees and began to gather their fruit—the big balls—as fast as possible. They were still plump enough to hold food-pulp. He realized that if he waited, they would probably dry up on their trees, shrivel to seed as the increasing cold drew the moisture from them. He spent that day in gathering a harvest, in piling great masses of the fruit in a small cavern-wall bubble near his sleeping chamber. When he had amassed enough to see him through at least two weeks, he gathered the fallen trunks and dried-up old stalks and piled them in the narrow entrance to this storage cave. He built a fire there, paced it out, and spread it out to burn slowly. He would have to keep this fire going and another like it in front of his own sleeping cavern.

He transferred the rabbits to his bubble-home also, rebuilding their pen.

As he had expected, the temperature in his hidden world continued its fall. A few days later it was quite chilly and the Moontrees had acted as he surmised. Their fruits had withered quite rapidly, finally dropping off as small hard seeds. The tree stalks dried out, turned hard, and fell. Robin gathered them as fuel for his fires, found that they were quite excellent, and also that the fresh-fallen ones could be woven into basketry.

The river continued to flow, but was more sluggish, and its waters began to grow cold. On the other hand, the Moonworms and other little creatures seemed to be having their heyday. They were out in quantities greater than he had ever seen and were busily gathering the fallen seeds, carrying them away, evidently preferring them to the fruit.

Robin made himself a jacket from an extra part of the padding, stitching it together with cord and thongs made from shell fibers. With a fire going at the door of his cave, he found he still wouldn't need blankets.

During the balance of the Lunar night Robin was forced to remain close to his caves, tending his fires, conserving all his energies. Outside, the temperature never actually reached freezing, or at least not that Robin could estimate. But at its worst, it was definitely chilly and the river fairly cold.

The view within the cavern cleared somewhat of its usual mugginess and he could see much more. He could now make out the walls on all sides, and discovered that the farthest distance, in the direction in which the river ran, was perhaps several miles off. The vegetation had mainly flattened, was drying up, and he could see everywhere the little ball-segmented insects humping and squirming about.

He saw a number of varieties he had not noticed before. One day venturing out with his bow and arrow, he disturbed something working amid a pile of broken stalks. The thing rushed out, directly at him. It was large, as large as a dog, and it ran straight for him silently, its wide mouth gaping.

He shot it, saw it fall over as it was about to leap at him. When he dug his arrow out, he saw that it was no wormlike insect, no segmented creature. It was a recognizable animal, a creature with two short stubby feet, two small extensions that were like hands on each side of an oval body. A definite head surmounted this, with one eerie eye set in the middle over its wide mouth. Two little breathing holes in the side attested to its possession of lungs. A long, curving rod grew out of the top of its skull and held a large yellow light-ball over it.

There was yet another peculiarity about this Moonhound, as Robin called it. It had no definite color. Its skin was faintly transparent, and he could see its inner organs shadowy within.

All this reminded Robin that there must be vast cavern worlds totally without light, yet having flora and fauna.

When there is no light, there is no need for pigmentation. Hence, this creature had none.

Robin also surmised that it was probably the cold that drove this beast into the lighted cavern in search of food, for he had never seen evidence of anything that large during the warm period.

Robin brought the carcass back to his cave and went to work to skin and cook it. At first he was not going to, for the hairless, colorless nature of it was rather repellent. But one thing Robin had learned long ago was not to let his emotions dictate to his needs. Like it or not, he was going to make use of everything here he could. He had a task, and that was to survive.

As a matter of fact, the meat cooked very nicely, turned brown in the fire, and tasted good. Further, it had a bone structure, which the Moonworms hadn't, and Robin saved these bones, knowing that there were many things that they could be used for. He remembered museum exhibits of bone needles, bone knives, and bone implements, including arrowheads and buttons that the Indians had made use of.

After that, Robin deliberately hunted for these Moonhounds and caught several others before the winter was over.

The warmth returned about when Robin had figured, starting a day or so after the surface sunrise. It rose rapidly, faster than it had fallen, and just as fast, new Moontrees were shooting up, new Moonmushrooms were growing, and the river was becoming warmer.

As time went on and month followed month, Robin found himself working into a comfortable, if primitive, routine. He charted exactly what to do on what days. He could tell in advance what he would be eating, what he would be harvesting. His rabbits had become sufficient in number to permit slaughtering, and he began to acquire a pile of rabbit furs. He found it no longer possible to keep all his rabbits in one pen, and finally liberated the majority of them and left them to shift for themselves. This worked out fine, and he never lacked the sight of at least one or two bunnies anywhere he looked. During the two weeks of winter each month they simply holed up as they might have done on Earth. It was an odd sight seeing the rabbits run wild, for their powerful leg muscles were many times stronger than was required by the weak gravity and, when they ran in a hurry, they would bounce many feet high in fantastic leaps.

Robin was now wearing a rabbit-fur outfit of coat, pants, and hat during the winter periods, equipped with bone buttons he'd carved from the Moonhound skeletons. He was, if anything, beginning to gain weight, but he was also aware of the paleness of his skin. He wondered whether staying in this sunless world a sufficient number of years would not make him as palely transparent as the Moonhounds.

But all this time Robin had not forgotten his ultimate mission—to reach the surface and signal for help. He had worked out the problem in his own mind. He had to make some sort of space suit, something that would permit him to venture out on the nearly airless surface long enough to set up a signal that astronomers might see.

He knew he had the materials for part of this suit in the metal salvaged from the rocket nose. He could polish a section sufficiently to make a heliograph with which he could flash a code message to any high-powered telescope that might be pointed his way. But he had also to fashion the metal into an airtight space helmet, and that he did not know how to do. The suit itself he could probably fashion from cloth and tanned skins, sew and seal it tight enough with animal fats and bone glue to be airtight for a short period, but he needed the helmet. He had the glass for it too, the little peepholes for the camera outlets and a large circular plate that had been set in the very base of the cargo nose and evidently intended for a wide-vision camera shot of the Earth. This plate would be his face plate.

Robin was aware of the hissing noise that he had first noticed on his arrival, but he had never investigated it. It was far off, somewhere along the wall of the cavern. One work period, when he found himself ahead of schedule, he set out to find the source of the noise.

Following the wall, with Cheeky running ahead chattering, the hiss gradually grew in volume. Robin made his way over a sharp cleft, skirted a large bubble-cave in the wall, and after about two miles of walking, came upon the source.

Issuing from a break in the outer cavern wall was a stream of blue flame. For several hundred feet around it no vegetation grew, the ground being covered with thin gray ash. Robin looked at the loudly hissing lance of blue fire.

It probably was a breakthrough from some adjoining bubble, one filled with a gas of some inflammable sort. Somehow in the course of the breakthrough, this leakage had been set aflame. And there it was now, a burning gas jet, sharp and hot.

At that moment, Robin knew he had the answer to his metalworking problem. He'd tried to melt the metal of the rocket over his fires but he had been totally unsuccessful. But this jet, this hot blue flame, this surely would do the trick!

For him the space helmet was now a certainty. It might take time, but now it could be done. That and more was possible, for he had enough metal to make a few necessities like a decent frying pan and a pot to use for boiling and perhaps a water container for a really long exploration trip.

That was the end of Robin's first "Stone Age" period and the beginning of his "Iron Age."

CHAPTER TEN
The Incredible Footprints

USING the gas jet proved to be considerably more difficult than might have been supposed. It was hard to approach too closely to the thing without running the danger of getting scorched. Also, to hold metal in it long enough to allow it to melt or become pliable it was necessary to find a way of holding the object without getting burned.

Robin did get several blisters before he finally worked out a system. Making himself a pair of thick rabbit-skin gloves lined with a thin coating of the ash from the area around the flame proved to be part of the solution. A pair of bone pliers proved to be another part, though the necessity of replacing these was continuous.

Working patiently then, Robin managed to cut and work some of the sheets of metal from the rocket nose. He made himself a hammer of hard stone with which to pound some shape into his pieces and finally had fashioned for himself a serviceable, though crude, frying pan and other implements he needed.

His next project was to be the space helmet, the first essential part of any space suit. He considered this a long time, planning just how to make it. He had a good sheet of metal for the job, but he didn't want to make any errors in working it, and he wanted to have as few seams as possible. Welding had thus far proved a task he had not mastered. He considered making the joints airtight by means of some sort of vegetable—or animal-fat product.

Robin sat in his cave watching the rebirth of life in the bubble-world after one of the winter half-months and thinking. He watched his monkey, Cheeky, turning over rocks for Moonworms—although the little brown pet had never been able to eat them, he seemed to enjoy the hunting of these odd creatures. He watched the rabbits bounding around, listened to those he kept penned up in the next cave.

"What am I waiting for?" he asked himself, half aloud. The monkey stopped at the sound of his voice, looked at him. Robin had developed the habit of talking to himself. He was aware of the danger that years of this hermit's life might well cause him to forget how to talk, and he did not want that. "I can't use a space suit until I can find a way to the surface—a safe way. And I've never even really explored this cavern itself. Maybe there's a simpler way of communication with the surface."

He sat and thought. The monkey dashed over to him, jumped on his knee, chattering. "I really ought to get about exploring this place," Robin went on. "You know, Cheeky, there might be some more things we can use. What do you say, shall we spend this next week playing Columbus, looking for more bubble worlds to conquer?"

The monkey chattered happily, jumped off his knee, and ran around. "Guess you like the idea," said Robin. "Let's get about it, then."

He got up and made his preparations. He filled a sack with enough food for several days. He took his homemade canteen, made from a hollowed-out Moontree fruit rind, filled it with water and hung it around his neck. He took his flashlight and knife, his bow and arrow, and his lantern of light organs. He had discovered that the little light-giving bulbs the animals carried would glow for about two days after their removal, and therefore he constantly kept this lantern refilled with his latest catches.

He looked to see whether his special lot of penned rabbits had enough food and water for the period and then, whistling to Cheeky, Robin set out. He went down to the bank of the flowing stream on which he had been originally carried and then set out to follow this rivulet its length into the distances of the bubble-world.

He followed the flowing stream for about twelve miles. The bubble widened out and the water, which had originally brushed the other side of the cavern where Robin had lived, had now narrowed as a bank of dry ground formed on the opposite side. Robin found himself walking through an ever deepening thicket of growing Moontrees which went on for many miles.

The stream twisted and moved off at right angles finally rushing into a deep pool. Robin went over and gazed into it. Plainly the pool had some sort of underground opening, for the water was swirling around with no visible surface outlet. So this was where the stream ran to! Doubtless it emptied into another bubble somewhere below, probably to fall like a waterfall into that space, there to become another stream and empty still again farther down until it ended in some vast reservoir of sub lunar seas.

But Robin was not interested in going farther down, he sought a way upward toward the surface, toward the sight of Earth. He turned away from the whirlpool, walked boundingly on to the farther wall of his home-bubble.

He reached it in time for his sleep period. It seemed as solid and impregnable as the wall around his home region.

Robin and Cheeky slept next to the wall and after their sleep resumed their search. Robin walked along the wall, looking again for some break. He saw in the distance a jagged line of black against the shining brown-gray of the cliff. When he reached it, it was a crack, a break in the surface of the bubble, reaching up several hundred feet. He came up to it.

It was wide, about ten feet wide, and dark. Robin shone his flashlight in, but as far as its rays could reach it was a dark tunnel. "Maybe this is what we're looking for," Robin said to Cheeky. "It seems to slant slightly upward. Maybe it will take us to the next bubble."

Cheeky peered in, walked in slowly and out of sight. "Hey," called Robin, "wait for me!" He followed the scampering monkey.

Now his lantern proved handy. The glow it shed could barely be noticed in the light of the great bubble, but here in the darkness of the cleft, the pale glow was distinct and definitely illuminated the ground a few feet in front of him. On he walked, holding the lantern ahead of him, watching Cheeky's long tail flick in and out of its circle of dim light, as the monkey would dash ahead and dash back.

Soon Robin found himself walking in almost total darkness, save for the limited glow of his lantern. The floor of the cleft occasionally slanted sharply, sometimes breaking steeply downward, sometimes necessitating jumps upward into the darkness. In the Moon's light gravity, Robin was a fantastic jumper, but the darkness made the problem very disconcerting. It was a strange thing to have to leap upward into a black void in hopes that what seemed like a wall in front of you would turn out to have a top and be but a giant step upward. He soared in the darkness, not knowing how near or how far the roof of the tunnel was, feeling strangely disembodied, the monkey clinging to his neck in transit.

He missed several such jumps, managed to avoid being bruised severely only by the feathery softness with which he fell afterward. When the going was straight, Cheeky would leap down and go ahead.

Suddenly he heard a screeching from the monkey.

He stopped, flashed his flashlight. The monkey was clutching the edge of a deep break, a pit cut sharply across the floor of the tunnel. Robin quickly reached the spot, scooped up Cheeky. His flashlight revealed the other side of the pit several yards away. Turning its rays downward, he could see no bottom to this crack within the tunnel. He shuddered, thinking what might have happened had he gone into it. Then, gathering Cheeky, Robin leaped.

He soared lightly across the abyss and landed safely on the other side. He went on, slowly, carefully.

A spot of light appeared before him. He stared at it and continued moving forward. The light widened, became the end of the tunnel, became the entrance to something new. He hastened on and burst at last into a new cavern-world, the world of the next bubble.

It looked much like his old one, but it was definitely smaller. The rounded ceiling could be made out quite clearly and he estimated its diameter as not more than a half mile. The far side of the bubble could be seen clearly and this one, he noticed, even from where he stood, had many such clefts and cracks in the wall. It was, he supposed, either an older bubble, more cracked in the course of eons of moon quakes and heat changes, or else it was more tightly knitted in a close mass of such bubbles.

A thick jungle of giant Moontrees was growing here, stalk-like plants resembling those he knew, but seemingly larger and more profuse. Robin started to walk through it toward the farther wall of the bubble. Cheeky had leaped into the stalks and was swinging through them ahead of him, when suddenly the monkey uttered a terrified shriek and there arose a strange high-pitched barking sound. Robin pushed through and saw the monkey, high in the top of a Moontree and a strange sort of Moonhound leaping for him. This kind of Moonhound was considerably bigger than the ones he had seen in his original bubble. It was uttering the eager bark of a hungry beast sighting its prey.

Robin unlimbered his bow and fitting an arrow into it, let fly. The sharp missile skewered the Moonbeast and the animal twisted in mid-air and fell thrashing to the ground. Robin dashed in and finished it off with a blow from the stone club he carried.

Cheeky came down from the tree cautiously, advanced to the dead animal, and prodded it. Then the monkey uttered a shriek, bared its teeth, and began to pommel the dead body as if he had been the one to bring it down.

Robin examined the animal. It was similar in many ways to the Moonhounds, yet different, and Robin's private theory that the Moonhound represented the equivalent of a mammal type seemed verified. Whereas the Moonhound was a wolf or dog, this creature corresponded more closely to a leopard or tiger.

The flesh of this creature seemed as if it might possibly make a substitute for leather—although it, too, was eerily transparent and it, too, possessed but one central eye and a large light organ.

Robin trekked on through this jungle until at last he reached the opposite wall. He was aware as he walked that there was a good deal of native life here, much more than had been evident in his own cavern. Evidently the first bubble was pretty much cut off from the general labyrinth of sublunar caverns. For as Robin walked, he caught glimpses of other Moonbeasts, slipping in and out, sometimes surprised and scurrying away. Moonworms, the equivalent of Earth's insect life, were here in plenty too, and there were many giant growths, which were different from those in his own cave, and some fruits of considerable promise were growing on them.

"We could do some farming now," said Robin to Cheeky. "I'll bring back some of the seeds from these bigger trees and plant them back home. It'll give us some variety."

The monkey merely chattered and pushed on ahead. At the farther wall, the original observation of many cracks was confirmed. The wall was broken like an eggshell and Robin could see that dozens of tunnels went out, probably leading to several other bubbles. He decided that the following day he would look for the ones that seemed to lead upward. But it was the time for sleep again.

He found a little cave, similar to the ones in which he had made his home, and there he and Cheeky ate their meal, cooking some of the meat from the Moontiger over a small open fire. The meat looked strange in its almost glassy appearance, yet it browned and tasted very good.

A thin stream of water meandered out of one of the cracks and from this Robin drank and refilled his canteen. He and the monkey curled up, now fed and contented, and went to sleep.

Robin awoke suddenly. He opened his eyes, puzzled. The monkey was screeching somewhere. He sat up, called, "Cheeky!"

The little creature dashed back to him. It had been outside the cave and it was excited. It was chattering and complaining as never before. The monkey jumped up and down in a perfect ecstasy of fury. Robin looked at it in wonder. He'd never seen Cheeky so excited. He sat up, looked around.

At first he saw nothing unusual. Outside the cave all was quiet. Then he noticed that his food pack had been moved. It had been dragged outside the cave, and its contents pulled out.

Robin got to his feet, went to it. Something had come into the cave silently, had taken the sack, and had examined its contents. He looked about, amazed and wondering.

Now he saw that other things had been touched. His canteen had been rolled over and the stopper unplugged. The water that had been inside was a little puddle on the cave floor.

Alarmed, Robin strung his bow, notched an arrow, and looked carefully around at the surrounding vegetation. Something was there, something big and cunning.

His eye's searched the ground and then he saw an outline in water from the canteen. Whatever it was had stepped into the puddle and then walked out of the cave. Robin saw a series of footprints.

Something that walked on two legs, something that took steps with a man-sized stride, something with three toes on each foot, that walked upright, was able to open bottles, look into sacks, and spy on sleeping strangers.

Something that might well be to the Moontiger and the Moonhound what Earth man was to the Earth tiger and the Earth hound. Moonman!

CHAPTER ELEVEN
The Glass Man

THE SITUATION was so astonishing that for a while Robin did not do anything but sit down inside his cave and catch his breath. Somehow he had assumed all along that he would not find anything on a human scale on the Moon. His life had been mainly confined to the first cavern-bubble he'd arrived at and this, as he now realized, had been a rather isolated one.

Unconsciously, he had assumed that life in other protected airtight sub lunar areas would be on a similarly low and limited level. Now he realized that he had had no right to make such an assumption. The Moon might harbor thousands and tens of thousands of bubbles; some might be hundreds of miles in scale; some, lower down, nearer the still-warm volcanic heart of the satellite, might even approach tropical climates and show little of the semi-monthly seasonal changes. In such places life might grow in profusion, might compel the kind of battle for existence as would bring out the evolution of a brain-carrying creature living on its wits.

And, although he was probably a little farther away from the central caverns at this moment, he was actually on the outskirts of the linked bubbles. In such border regions he might indeed encounter rovers and wanderers from the more prolific areas.

But the problem was now how to find this prowler. There was, he hoped, only one of them. The creature was probably hanging around somewhere, even now, keeping an eye on Robin's doings.

Robin got to his feet, looked through his provisions. He found a bit of rabbit meat, took it out, and skewered it on a cooking stick. He then knelt inside his cave-refuge and built a fire, using his flint and steel. Over this fire he hung the bit of meat and set it to roasting. He carefully began to fan the smoke out of the cave, knowing that it would carry the new and tongue-tempting odor of cooked meat to everything in the vicinity.

Robin slipped out of the cave and hid himself in a thick clump of growth nearby. Cheeky clung to his shoulder, hushed to silence. They waited.

After a few minutes Robin saw a slight motion in the vegetation at the other side of the cave entrance. He watched, and a moment later saw a head thrust itself out, and then a figure emerge and silently stalk to the cave and look in. It was manlike, walking on two feet and it had two arms. It was oddly misty, seeming naked and semi-transparent like the other animal life.

In one hand the creature carried a long stick to which something sharp and glassy was attached—clearly a type of spear. The creature paused at the cave mouth, then seeing no one within and unable to resist the tantalizing curiosity of cooking meat and a small fire, it went inside.

Immediately Robin dashed out of hiding, ran across the small space and blocked the entrance of the cave with his body. The creature within was bending over the meat, but on hearing Robin, it turned, and made a wild dash for the cave mouth.

It collided with Robin. For a moment there was a wild scramble of arms and legs and then Robin's greatly superior Earth muscles overpowered the other's and the creature was caught. Robin held it tightly in his arms, carried it into the cave, and sat it down.

The spear had been knocked aside in the tussle and Robin looked at it with a glance. One glance was enough to make the young man realize that he had had a narrow escape. Its tip was bright and as sharp as a piece of broken glass. If the creature had thought to jab that spear, it might have been deadly.

But now the captured being was sitting quietly in a sort of resignation, merely looking at Robin with the same curiosity that Robin bestowed upon it. It was very much like a human being, perhaps some four feet tall. But its head was somewhat triangular in shape, having only one eye (Robin never found any Moon creatures with two), and was topped with a large yellow light bulb that extended a foot above.

Robin took the bit of meat, cut off a piece and held it out to the creature. The Moonman looked at it, then reached out a hand and took it. It smelled it, then tasted it, and, finding the taste to its liking, swiftly gobbled it down.

Robin ate some too, and this gesture seemed to reconcile the other. A fairly universal gesture, Robin thought. Only friends would share a meal. Probably would hold true anywhere in the universe.

Now Robin picked up the other's spear and examined it. Seeing this, the creature picked up one of Robin's sacks and also looked at it.

The sharp point of the spear was something that looked like glass but glistened far more, seemed sharper, harder, and heavier. Robin turned it over, and the realization struck him that this spearhead was a diamond, a single six-inch-long shard of diamond!

After the first shock of this discovery, Robin realized that he should have expected it. On such a volcanic world as the Moon had once been, there might well be lots of diamond in great masses. What could be easier to use for weapons and cutting edges than chunks broken from such masses. Such a chunk brought back to Earth might be worth an emperor's ransom—but who could think of such values here?

Getting the friendship of the Moonman proved to be easy after that first effort. For the creature made no further effort to escape, seemed itself to desire Robin's companionship. In fact, as it turned out, Robin would have had a hard time getting rid of it. It seemed anxious now to stay close to the Earthling, to share him with Cheeky.

The glass-skinned being had a language, for it soon began to jabber away at Robin in a high-pitched squeaky tongue. After a little experimentation, Robin was able to get it to repeat the name Robin, and in turn, he found out that the Glassie's own name was something nearly like Korree.

Korree was evidently a very primitive sort of savage in spite of his ability to speak. As Robin set out to recross this bubble and return to his own holdings, the creature wound in and out ahead of him, returning steadily to see if all was well. Korree had no clothes and no understanding of them. He had only his spear, which Robin had returned to him and he had apparently lost faith in that, the first time Robin used his bow and arrow on a yapping Moontiger.

The trip through the dark tunnels back to Robin's original bubble was comparatively easy, for no sooner did they get into the darkness than Korree's light organ began to glow brightly enough to render Robin's lantern dim. When they came to the cleft, Robin had to pick the Moonman up and jump with him, for Korree's muscles were built only for Moon gravity and that leap was beyond his normal ability.

Once back in what Robin now thought of as the safety of his original bubble, the two settled down to work together. Korree soon got the hang of the simple duties Robin gave him—feeding the rabbits, slaughtering, skinning, and tanning. They spent the time trying to learn each other's languages.

Robin carefully jotted down each new sound or word he could identify in the Glassie's speech and Korree in turn seemed anxious to imitate the English.

It took about four months before they had a working interchange of ideas. Robin found that the Glassie's language was quite limited in many ways, though having a great many variations of verb form—a typical character-istic of primitive tongues. Finally, however, Robin heard Korree's story.

His people lived many bubbles away, possibly many months of travel, though the Glassie idea of time was very vague and seemed hedged around by all sorts of untranslatable mystic conditions. There were maybe several hundred of them and they formed one big tribe or family.

There were many such tribes, usually one to a bubble-cavern. Korree indicated that somewhere—he pointed downward—were greater caverns where many tribes lived, tribes of great strength or magic or knowledge. Robin could not decide which was meant—probably all three. But Korree had never been there. These downward regions were taboo to his people.

Robin's suspicion was that the Glassies from Korree's group had been forced to live in the less desirable outer areas by the stronger and more advanced races who had seized the better regions.

Korree indicated that there were many bubbles that were not inhabited because of great terrors, either by heat or cold. Robin assumed he meant caverns of jungle and caverns more exposed to the surface temperatures.

Korree himself had broken some sort of tribal rule or magic and had been chased out of his home. He was a lonely outcast. That was why he had gone with Robin when Robin had given him food. This symbolized acceptance into Robin's tribe. And though Robin looked to him like a very strange sort of man indeed—a solid man, a "rock" man was the way Korree explained Robin's nontransparent flesh and his tremendous strength—Korree had been glad to find acceptance anywhere.

Carefully questioning Korree about the surface, Robin found that the Glassie had apparently no conception of what sort of a world the Moon really was. To him it was a place of many enclosed spaces. The surface he had neither seen nor even dreamed of. That there could be a place where the enclosures ended and the world "dropped off" into nothing, this was something he could not imagine.

Robin then asked questions about the upward regions. Korree indicated that these were less and less habitable, that his people strove always to go down, never up. Robin twisted his questions around, trying to determine if the Glassies had ever seen anything that might signify the surface. He described the sun and the Earth to Korree but the Glassie seemed unable to understand. But when he spoke of the sun as being a bright glowing thing so bright that it hurt the eyes to look at it, Korree seemed to remember something.

Carefully the Glassie told Robin that he had heard of a tribe that lived somewhere in the upper regions, where in one part of their bubble there sometimes came a terrible white-hot light that hurt when one looked upon it. This light was not always there, but shone through the top of the cavern, which Korree explained was like the substance of his arm—that is, semi-transparent.

Robin became very excited when he heard this. It sounded to him as if somewhere up near the surface there must be an airtight cleft or bubble whose outer crust might be natural volcanic glass. Through this the sun might sometimes penetrate to produce the phenomenon Korree described.

Plainly then, this was the place Robin must find. It looked like the ideal place to begin his projected signaling to Earth. But whether it was or not, Robin would have to make a visit there to see.

Korree did not like the idea, but indicated he would be willing to go along. "Could you lead me there?" Robin asked.

"Much hard," Korree replied. "Can make do. You-me not like. Many-winter trip, many bubbles."

But Robin was determined. "We will go. First I must make a space suit. I may need it." Korree spread out a hand in acceptance.

It took about two months more to finish what Robin hoped would be a workable space suit. The helmet he finally managed to weld into something like a practical shape. It fitted over his head snugly, the little glass plate in front of his eyes. Its seams were closed as best as could be managed and sealed with melted animal fat. The bottom of the helmet fitted snugly over Robin's shoulders and would be attached to baggy leather arm-and-hand coverings. The bottom of Robin's body would be simply encased in several layers of clothing made as airtight as possible.

To carry a supply of air, Robin fashioned a large sack of Moonhound skins, which, when filled with air and brought to the surface of the Moon, would swell up like a huge balloon. He hoped that by breathing from this reserve he might be able to survive on the surface for perhaps twenty or thirty minutes. This would be all he would need, he estimated, to rush out, set up some sort of reflector or flare if he could contrive such, and dash back to safety. "Safety" would, of course, be some previously sealed dome extending to the surface, through which he could cut a space narrow enough to leave, and yet, one which would not be entirely exhausted of its inner gases by the time Robin got back to reseal it.

This was a long-chance project, yet it was the only hope Robin could think of. The matter could at least be examined at closer range if he could but find the cavern with the translucent roof. This would be an ideal base for his project.

Robin packed his equipment, liberated the last of his penned rabbits, and loaded as much food as he could in big sacks which he and Korree carried. Then, preceded again by Cheeky's monkey bounds, Robin turned his back on his "home" and headed back to the tunnel and the caverns beyond.

It had been over a year and a half since he had been cast away on the Moon, perhaps nearer two years. And now he was ready at long last to begin the long trek home.

CHAPTER TWELVE
The Long Trek

As THEY PROGRESSED, Robin queried Korree as best he could as to the exact location of this fabled place from which the sun could be seen. "I not know from here," the Glassie replied. "Go from home place, yes. We go Korree home place first."

Robin thought about that as they trudged along. He went easily and lightly in spite of his huge load—a collection of sacks and equipment tied together to make a bundle more than his own height. But bundle and all, Robin was lighter and stronger by far than he would be on Earth. "Won't they kill you if you go back?" he asked the Moonman.

Korree turned his head and Robin almost imagined he could see his brains whirl. Through the glassy skin, he could see the shadows of his skull structure and the pulsing of veins and arteries. "With Robin they not do so. You make them give us free way." Obviously he regarded the Earthling as an all-powerful being to whom things like tribal death sentences would be mere nothings.

Robin smiled uneasily. Without firearms and modern weapons he could still be overpowered if enough of the Moonmen attacked him at once. He would have to think about his approach to the tribe before he got there.

They reached the tunnel and made their way once more through its dark recesses to the jungle-bubble where he had encountered Korree. They passed through this without incident. The Glassie led the way to one of several cracks and tunnels at the far end. With Robin following and the monkey Cheeky perched on the huge pack, Korree entered this tunnel.

As before, it was dark and narrow and seemed to wind ahead. Several times they stepped around breaks in the floor, or ducked under low passages where the ceiling had dipped. They walked on, Korree's bobbing headlight casting a pale-yellowish glow a few feet ahead. Robin was watching the floor carefully, straining his attention to keep his footing safe. His ears registered the echo of their motions and the changing pitch as the tunnel widened or receded, but he paid less and less attention to this.

Suddenly he looked up. And saw not the one glow of Korree's light but a number of smaller ones around them, distant ones, bobbing slightly, one or two yellow, one small white one, and three verging on red. He started and stared but Korree had said nothing.

Finally he reached out and tapped the Glassie and whispered, "What are those lights?"

Korree said back in a normal tone, "Animals White light is hunting eater. I watch it."

"Here? In this tunnel?" asked Robin, startled.

"Not in tunnel," said the Glassie. "In new bubble-place."

Robin looked around. Sure enough he had not noticed the echo of their feet in the last few minutes. The floor had changed from rock to sandy dirt and he realized that he had lost some of the enclosed-air feeling. It was indeed a new bubble-cavern—but a lightless one!

Now, as he looked carefully, he realized that there were many lights around. There were tiny ones bobbing on the ground that were probably Moonworms. The others were almost certainly those of various animals. He took his flashlight out, suddenly clicked it on, and swung it around.

They were in an open area, sandy with sparse clumps of mushroom-like vegetation growing here and there. He caught the scurrying flash of several translucent animal bodies dodging out of sight from the unexpected light of his flash. And when the beam was off, he noticed the headlights returning, augmented in number.

"There are many bubble-places without light?" asked Robin.

"Many," said Korree. "Glassies not live there, but many animals hunt there."

Robin wondered whether there might in fact be more bubbles without light than with. He realized that that was probably the case; it very likely explained the nearly complete lack of pigment in the flesh of the native animals, the presence of the light stalks on all of them. It had probably evolved originally in lightlessness, and the Glassies had moved into the caverns fortunate enough to have natural phosphorescence only after they had discovered them much later in their history. This possibly also accounted for the single eye of Moon creatures—the conditions for the use of two eyes to develop perspective and delicate differentiations of shading and coloring simply never existed.

"Are there animals here without eye or light?" asked Robin thoughtfully.

"Yes," Korree answered softly. "Big eaters, they—" There was a sudden rush of sound ahead, a crashing of plants nearby, an instant winking out of all headlights, including Korree's, and then Robin felt himself thrown to the ground as something vast and huge and heavy seemed to envelop him.

He felt himself being smothered under a pulsing blanket of warm flesh, a veritable wall that covered him from head to foot, crushing out his strength. Robin recovered, ripped out with his hands, kicked with his feet. He felt his strong Terrestrial muscles tearing into the tissue of the creature, and swinging wildly. He got to his knees and then to his feet, veritably lifting the entire bulk of the creature.

He reached for his knife and as he got it open he felt the sharp edge of a jaw and the hot breath of a large mouth near his ear. He thrust out with the knife hard and furiously, cutting the mass to bits.

There was a sharp screech and he felt the blanket of flesh pull away and struggle to withdraw. He got his flashlight with his other hand, flicked it on to see his opponent better.

He saw a wall of gelatinous flesh rolling back before him. It rolled off the prostrate but unharmed body of Korree, gathered itself in a mass and rolled rapidly away, uttering loud screeches. The thing was a ball of flesh, several yards across. It had a wide, many-toothed mouth. It had several flat flanged spots, which were probably, ears, and it was lacking an eye, lacking any light organ.

It hardly needed them. Obviously the thing simply rolled around in the darkness of the cavern, guided by the sounds of moving animals, rolling over them, flattening out, and devouring them.

Korree got to his feet. He said nothing, seemed to take it for granted that the great Earthling would have bested this thing, of course, and started off again. Robin frowned, decided he'd have to watch himself lest the Glassie sometime really overestimate his capacities.

They traversed the rest of the lightless cavern without incident, this time Robin keeping his flashlight switching on and off regularly, long enough to sweep the moonscape sufficiently to gain warnings of future assaults. Once they saw the ball-like bulk of a Moonbowler, as Robin mentally named it, in the distance, and they both carefully stopped and held their breath until it rolled away.

At the far wall, Korree searched the various breaks until he found the one through which he had originally come.

They passed through another lightless cavern, this one less of a desert than the other, where giant mushrooms towered like great trees in the darkness and where little chittering Moonmice ran about their feet, tiny green lights sparkling.

The next cavern was a lighted one and this was now almost familiar to them. Beyond that was another lighted one through which a channel of water flowed only to disappear into a tiny crack in the far wall. This water, however, was yellowish and evil-smelling and made the entire cavern malodorous. Yet it too had its quota of strange vegetation.

A series of rather small bubbles, not more than a couple of dozen yards across, came next, and then they arrived at a wide, deep one. The spot in the wall, which let out on it was near the roof of this bubble, and they made their way delicately along a series of faults and ledges. Looking down, Robin could see that a lake of some bubbling oily substance filled the lower level of the bubble. Along one side, tucked in a corner near a tunnel opening, many hundreds of feet down, he spotted something odd. He stopped. Korree turned back, made his way along the narrow ledge and looked down to where he pointed.

There was a small cleared space just before the opening, and there were several objects too far away to be seen clearly, but they looked for all the world like some sort of eggs. As they watched, Robin saw what seemed a shadowy figure move near one. Because of the curious glassy skins, that was probably an animal. Robin softly asked Korree what it was.

"Is Glassie like Korree," answered Korree quietly.

"A friend? One of your people? And what are they doing there?" asked Robin.

Korree shook his head violently. "Not Korree people. That one is from down place. Is mighty people from…" He pointed downward to the Moon's core. "They come here to take…" He pointed now at the curious chemical lake. "They bring back down with them," he finished.

Robin gasped. Here was evidence of his reasoning.

The Glassies that lived near the core of the Moon were higher in civilization. Here evidently was a place where something usable could be gathered—the fluid of that lake. Possibly it might be fuel for burning, or substance usable as tar or cement. The beings down below came up for it, put it in tanks—the egg-shaped objects—and brought it back to their greater caverns.

Someday this would have to be investigated. If he ever returned to Earth, this would have to be explored. But now—were these unknowns dangerous to him? He asked Korree, who shrugged. In his halting fashion he conveyed to the Earthling that if the Glassies of the upper crust left those lower down alone, they were not bothered. The implication however was that Korree's people were only too willing to stay out of the way of the powerful underlords.

After several more caverns—the trip had already taken over a week—including one marvelous one in which several flaming gas jets made amazing patterns in an otherwise lightless world, Korree finally led the way into a large lighted cavern many miles wide, stopped and announced, "Korree home."

Robin looked around, adjusted his pack and called to Cheeky to return. The monkey, which had scampered on ahead, obediently dashed back and to safety on the pack. This was an important moment to Robin. He mustered his plans, and stepped out after Korree who had started out again holding his spear high in the air in some sort of native signal.

For a short while they walked without seeing anyone. They were in a forest of ball-trees when suddenly they found themselves quietly surrounded by Glassies. Evidently they had been trailed since entering the cavern and at a sufficient distance from the tunnel mouth the Glassies had popped out of concealment.

There were about twenty or so, all armed with the diamond spears and they effectively encircled the travelers. Korree had apparently expected this, for he showed no surprise, but Robin stopped short and Cheeky started jumping up and down on the huge pack and shrieking at the pack of beings.

It was odd seeing a mass of Glassies. Robin could see that they differed from each other as individuals. Some were larger, some smaller, and the shadings within their bodies gave rather clear evidence of fatness, of recent eating, and such. Like Korree they wore no garments at all.

One of the Glassies said something sharply to Korree, who answered promptly. The spokesman had a black circle painted on his chest—this was obviously a symbol of some sort of tribal authority. Robin stepped forward, walked up to this Glassie, who promptly withdrew, uneasy in the presence of this unknown.

From his pocket Robin took his pack of matches, the one that had been with him all the way from Earth. There were still three matches left, saved for just some occasion as this, carefully conserved by the use of Robin's flint and steel. Robin walked up to a small ball-tree nearby, held the match aloft, then struck it, and rapidly held it to the stalk-like trunk. After a second the plant caught fire and was a blazing mass.

While the Glassies were gazing in amazement at this unexpected display, Robin drew in his breath, set his pack down, and gave a leap straight upward with all his strength.

He soared some thirty feet high and then gently floated down to the ground again. This was a feat that anyone with Earth muscles could do, but it was something that Lunar muscles had never been developed for. When the Glassies tore their eyes away from the burning tree it was to find Robin apparently vanished. Looking around, one of them discovered him in the air, floating gently back to the ground.

With one accord the Glassies shrieked and ran away. When Robin hit the ground, he was alone with Korree—who looked as nearly smug as it was possible for his unearthly features to look.

The Earthling picked up his sack, whistled to Cheeky to come to him, and started off again. In a few minutes, Korree led him to the tribal center, the "village" of his people.

There were no houses or tents or any structures with roofs. Each family group apparently fenced off their section of ground with a barrier of low, pointed sticks, their points diagonally outward. Within this barrier, the family squatted with their few possessions. There was no such thing as privacy among this primitive group. The females of the tribe apparently stayed within their family plots, with the young, the extra spears and hunting sticks, the leftover supplies of food, and a pile in the center of each circle of what must have been some sort of blankets, apparently woven crudely from vegetable fibers. Robin assumed that during the cold periods, these were used.

The males of the tribe were gathered before a central circle, watching their visitors approach. Korree went to them, stopped, and spoke at length. Robin could not understand him, but he knew what he must be saying. His Glassie friend was obviously first boasting of his friendship with the magical stranger, then warning them of terrible consequences if they failed to obey and honor the stranger, doubtless inserting a demand for his own full pardon of whatever tribal offense had brought about his own banishment, and demanding the aid of the tribal leaders in assisting them on their way.

When he had finished, Robin walked straight up to the Glassie with the chest marking, reached out and extracted from the tip of his quivering light-organ stalk a copper cent, which Robin had first palmed in his hand. To the astonished native, he presented this token—one of the coins Robin had had in his pocket on his unexpected trip from New Mexico.

The Glassie took it, stared at it. The face on the coppery-yellow coin seemed to hypnotize him. No one had ever seen such a thing—a bit of bright rock with a face on it! But this additional evidence of Robin's magic clinched the argument.

Robin and Korree stayed in that cavern for about three days. In that time Korree managed to obtain fairly specific directions from one old-timer as to the cavern they sought. He had also evidently repaired his tribal fences, for Robin could not fail to notice that Korree was always accompanied by a group of anxious and placating Glassies. He imagined that when Korree returned to stay, it would be as a chieftain.

The nature of the tribe's culture remained much of a mystery. They were very primitive, yet they seemed to have a complicated series of taboos and ceremonies. There was clearly a very definite code of marriage and family relations, though its limitations were puzzling.

Robin discovered something about them, however. One of the circular enclosures was apparently a tribal storehouse, or temple, or arsenal, or magic circle— exactly what he could not tell—save that no family lived within and there were little piles of oddities carefully placed inside its magic circle. The penny Robin had "pulled from the chief's head" reposed therein on a raised mound. The burnt match stick lay beside it. The rest of the contents seemed to be curiously shaped stones, odd bits of animal skin, a skeleton of something big and round which might perhaps have been that of a Moonbowler slain by the hero of the tribe. Several diamond spearheads were there, including some that had fractured in use. And something that glistened like metal.

Robin saw this latter, and, stepping boldly inside the magic circle, picked this object up and examined it. It was a knife blade!

It was nothing of Terrestrial manufacture. It was about nine inches long and a couple of inches wide at the hilt, tapering down to a point. It was edged on one side, and bore the marks of having been hammered down and shaped by a hand mallet rather than ever having felt the heat of a forge. Engraved in its rather soft white metal were a series of odd hooks and lines that looked like writing of a sort. The hilt end was jagged as if the blade had been snapped off in careless usage.

Robin called to Korree and asked him about the object. Korree consulted with the chief and returned. "Sharp thing, it come from down-there people," he said, pointing to the regions below. "Glassie of those die in break of tunnel. We find, take this."

Well, Robin thought, this adds to the evidence. There is some sort of higher civilization below. Not yet at the fire-building stage, but advancing at the dawn of the Iron Age. I wonder if this is really writing or just a design? And I wonder what metal this is? Not iron surely.

He thought a while, then deciding that as a creature of magic he could get away with it, informed Korree that he would take the knife blade away with him. The Glassies seemed unconcerned. It was evident that Robin was far outside their taboos.

The question of time among the Glassies was an odd one. The Earthling had surmised as much in his observations of Korree. There seemed to be no effort to divide the periods into rest and work. Some hunted and worked when they felt like it, others slept at the same time.

When the time came, Robin and Korree made their way out of the cavern upward along a ledge on one side of the bubble wall, through a fault higher up and began to climb a sloping tunnel.

For several more days they traveled, always working upward, passing through bubbles of gradually diminishing diameter and sparser vegetation. At one point they waded through a shallow pond, at another they choked in a sulfury cloud of gas that hung about. They squeezed through ever tighter cracks, and the air began to get distinctly thinner and harder to breathe. They were both getting exhausted quite easily; Robin knew they were nearing the surface and the spongy mass of the Moon's interior was tightening.

Then at last they stood in a tiny spherical bubble and gazed at a pool of brackish water at one end. There were no cracks in this little cave, no further tunnel or means of progress. "What now?" asked Robin, turning to his companion. Had they taken the wrong turn and come to a dead end?

Korree went over to the water pool. He gestured at it, made motions of holding his breath. "We go down in here, move under and come up...out." He waved a hand in a down-and-under gesture. Robin looked into the water. Maybe the Glassie was right. It was possible that the water at the bottom passed into a fault and led into another cavern. But could he risk it?

Korree nodded and without another word, suddenly jumped into the water, spear and all, and vanished. Robin waited. In a little while Korree's head appeared again and the Glassie climbed out. "Tunnel over there," he said, waving beyond the wall of the bubble. "Go up sharp."

Well, there was nothing to do but to try it. Robin set down his pack and thought a moment. Cheeky the monkey was scampering around the floor of the small bubble. Robin took off his jacket and shoes, took out of his pocket anything that might be damaged by water, and leaped into the pool.

It was an eerie sensation. The water was as dense as on Earth but its weight was so much less. It seemed almost to lack substance as Robin pushed through it, dived deep, and let himself come up again as far as possible.

He broke water in total darkness. He was outside the cavern, but exactly where he could not tell. Korree with his light organ had known and that was sufficient. Robin reached for a bank, felt a sloping wall. He grabbed it, pulled himself up in the darkness. That much was right. There was a tunnel here running steeply upward. He sniffed the air. It was strange—breathable, but strange. This part of the Moon enclosure was certainly cut off from the other sections…that was certain.

Robin let himself back into the water, swam for the cavern, and came up in it. He got hold of Cheeky, opened his pack, and extracted his homemade space helmet. He stuffed the monkey into it, closed end upward, and got into the water again. Moving swiftly under water, the terrified animal clutching the inside of the helmet, Robin transferred him to the other side, found a small level section by probing around, and deposited the helmet. He returned for the rest of his pack by this method, and finally everything was complete again in the new passage. By the light of Korree's head, he saw that they were in a narrow tunnel angling steeply upward. Robin's clothes and the pack had dried with great speed in the thin air and the low gravity. They made their way up this passage with difficulty and at last found themselves facing a lighted opening.

They emerged into a new cavern, but one quite different from those that had gone before. It was long, perhaps two or three miles long, but narrow, not more than a hundred feet or so at the widest. Looking upward, the steep perpendicular walls seemed to come together and closed up tightly about a quarter of a mile high.

A faint phosphorescence dimly lighted the new area. As they walked on, Robin became aware that there was no vegetation here that his feet were moving through light dust. He let it run through his fingers. It felt chalky as pumice.

He looked around them again and then he realized that he had at last reached the surface of the Moon. He was walking through the bottom of a long crack in the surface, a cleft that had somehow closed up again to preserve a cache of air. But this dust, this was the surface dust of Luna, fallen to the bottom of the cleft!

As they walked, the dimness seemed to diminish. A whitish glow began to envelop them. Robin blinked at the strange light. Things began to take on strange colorations that he had not noticed before. He looked upward and saw that the ceiling of the cleft no longer was bathed in blackness. Instead there seemed a break there, a glassy glimmer through which poured a dazzling white light.

Somewhere up there the crack had been sealed by volcanic action into grayish natural glass. Somewhere outside the sun was shining down upon the Moon. Its rays were bathing the surface above the concealed cleft and some were finding their way down. For the first time in many long and difficult months Robin felt warmth and light together. He had reached the sunlight!

CHAPTER THIRTEEN
The Sun and the Trap

THERE HAD BEEN a distinct chill in the strange surface canyon, but from the moment that the white sunlight began to stream in, there was a definite warming effect. The rays were diffused by the substance above, which sealed the cleft, yet the sun was strong while it lasted. Robin felt good as he bathed in its rays. He looked at himself, at Korree, in wonder.

For the clear white light was the first normal lighting he had seen in all the time he had been marooned below. Now he received the first true color visualization of himself and his companion. He saw from his hands that he had become very pale-skinned; all his normal tan had been lost in the cavern worlds. He unpacked the bright, gleaming space helmet and used it as a makeshift mirror. His hair had faded to a light blond, and there were several white hairs now visible, the result presumably of his period of exposure to the unshielded rays of the sun during his passage through space.

In the clear light Korree seemed even more transparent than ever, and indeed Robin could make out the shadowy, pulsating shapes of his internal organs quite clearly—his skeleton standing out sharply. He realized how dim and abnormal the phosphorescence of the caverns had really been.

Reshouldering his pack, they continued up the deep canyon. In a little while, the gray ashy surface gave way to sandy soil and there was a dampness in the air that indicated the presence of one of the deposits of water. Now the familiar Lunar vegetation was making its presence known and before long they were wandering through a very dense thicket of huge ball-trees and plants.

Robin had never seen such a dense jungle growth on the Moon before and he attributed it to the occasional bath of sunlight this one cavern received. It was like a hothouse, a natural one, more or less sealed with a high dampness, natural warmth augmented by screened sunlight.

Soon the two found themselves forcing their way single file through the growth, while Cheeky swung into the tops and made his own way, happy in the sort of thick, warm forest his monkey nature demanded. Robin pushed his way through first, with Korree following in the path the Earthling cleared.

Robin went on through the jungle, struggling in spite of his powerful Earth muscles to push his pack along. After a while he stopped to rest, looked back. He saw behind him only the bruised and broken stalks of the ball-trees he'd passed through. There was no sign of Korree.

Robin stared, but the forest was too thick to allow much vision. He set the pack down, called, "Korree!"

There was no answer. Somewhere in the distance a stalk snapped. Robin called again. Still no answer. He started back a few steps, retracing his path, but there was still no sign of his Glassie friend.

He suddenly felt uneasy. What was going on here? How had his companion vanished? He went back to where he had left his pack, waited, again calling his friend's name. But still there was no answer. There were more crackling noises somewhere in the thick vegetation. Perhaps Korree was in trouble there?

Robin turned in that direction, started to push through the barrier of tree stalks. Suddenly there was a rushing noise, a chorus of shrieks all around, and something heavy fell around him.

He whirled, but something sticky and tight was encircling his body. He caught glimpses of glasslike, one-eyed faces jumping around him, hiding in the branches, shrieking. He struggled again to free himself but the encircling Glassies threw more of the sticky ropes around him, more things like barrel staves that fell and tied him up.

He struggled to use his full strength against them but his arms were pinned to his sides, he was tight amid the stalks and he could not brace himself. Fight as he might, he was caught, and he saw that there were stalk-ropes attached to those that had trapped him and these were being further secured by the creatures around him.

He stopped struggling, quieted. It was obviously no use to waste his strength. Let's see what they intend to do next, he thought.

For a while they did nothing. Then his Glassie captors—he still could see little of them so thick was the jungle—seemed to be working their way together so that all their attached ropes were soon leading off in the same direction. Then they started to pull.

Had Robin chosen to resist it might have become a fruitless tug of war, but he did not. He had decided that his best course was to go along with them. Doubtless they would lead him to their village or at least to an open space where his great Earth strength might then come into better play.

For a while, therefore, he allowed himself to be led through the Moontree forest, dragging himself enough to give his captors a workout. Robin had cagily decided that the more tired they were when they finally arrived, the better for him.

After a time the thicket of plants came to an end and Robin found himself, as he had presumed, at the native settlement. Unlike the ones he had seen in Korree's home cavern, these Glassies were cavemen. They evidently made their homes in a section of this narrow surface-cleft where one of the walls was greatly pocked with holes and openings. The cliff walls were apparently quite like pumice here. Under the circumstances and because of the limited width of the area, it was quite logical that the inhabitants should have made use of these holes.

There were several dozen such cave entrances and Robin could see a fair number of Glassies around them, including women and young ones. His captors, he now saw, numbered about fifteen, all male hunters like Korree. They hustled him along to a central cave, whose entrance was decorated with blue circles, clearly the designation of their chief.

Korree was already there, tied, as was Robin. He looked relieved to see the Earthling, and also a little puzzled at seeing that Robin too was a prisoner

"They catch me when Robin not looking," he said, explaining the obvious. "I not like these Glassies' ways. I think they mean kill."

Robin looked around at them. "We'll see. Back in my land, we have a saying, 'There's many a slip between the cup and the lip.' I think we will get away. Wait and watch."

Korree immediately showed relief. He had a profound faith in Robin's magical abilities. To him, therefore, Robin's lack of fright was enough evidence that all was really well.

The band gathered before the chief's cave was waiting. Presently a voice came from the cave darkness. It questioned one of the captors, who turned and repeated the query to Korree. Korree answered at length, and his answer in turn was repeated into the cave.

At Robin's query, Korree said that he had just informed the hidden chief that Robin was a great man-beast who would destroy them all if he was not immediately released and placated.

More cave talk and interchange. There was a delay for awhile and Robin could faintly hear voices within the cave, as if the chief were discussing the matter with someone else. Then a command was issued. The captors pulled on the ropes and urged Korree and Robin to the door of another cave. They pushed them into this and rolled a large boulder in front of the cave mouth to block their exit.

It was dark inside the cave but not so dark that they could not see that it was about twenty feet long and that there were a number of piles of stuff around, food possibly, or remnants of things. Korree and Robin eased themselves down on the hard floor.

Robin studied the vegetable cords that bound him. He twisted his hands and pulled until he got his elbow up where he could exert pressure. Then he strained against one of the bonds. In a few seconds it parted and broke. In this way he snapped bond after bond until he was free. He was sticky from them, for the stalks had been soaked in some sort of adhesive substance, which had made them so effective. But the strength of Earth muscles was more than they had ever held before.

Next Robin went to work on Korree's bonds and broke them off one by one. The two silently stretched their cramped bodies. Korree glanced back at the dark end of the cave and his headlight organ glowed brightly for a moment. Something among the bundles was stirring slightly. Korree said quietly, "Another prisoner or a listener?"

Robin looked. Yes, there was something over there, apparently tied up also. It might be a Glassie prisoner, or it might be some one of his captors trying to spy on them. He shrugged. Let them try. They couldn't understand English.

The two sat down near the entrance, conversed quietly. Korree was of the opinion that the Glassies would eventually kill them in some sort of ceremony. Robin never had found out how different tribes of Glassies acted toward each other. Evidently they did not make war, but neither did they have much contact or exchange. In general, they treated each other like suspicious strangers, avoiding contact whenever possible. But it seemed now that when strangers did force their way into unwelcome tribal caverns, death was the result. This was fairly typical of the most primitive savages on Earth and it was evidently a rule for that level of culture anywhere in the universe.

For a while then they sat silently, thinking about their plight. Robin, somehow, was not too worried. He had become so used to the superiority of his muscles that he felt that he could eventually manage his escape when the time came. The question was, where could he escape to? This particular region was not actually a part of the honeycomb of Luna's interior—it was a cleft sealed in by a trick of volcanic fate on the very surface. Probably it had no other exit than the one that led into it.

Again, escape though he might, could he save Korree too? He thought about it in silence. Korree broke the meditations. "Have hunger. Is food here?"

"There must be some around," said Robin, glancing back at the things in the rear of their prison-cave. The figure back there stirred a bit. And then there was a mumbling sound and a voice said something. The voice was deep and strong, unlike the sound of a Glassie's tongue. But Robin could not understand it. Korree too looked and listened.

"Did you understand him?" Robin asked his companion.

Korree shook his head. Now at the sound of Robin's words occurred the most astonishing surprise that Robin had yet encountered. The unseen speaker spoke again:

"Who is that? Is there someone here who speaks English?"

It was a human voice! It spoke Robin's language, though the intonation and accent were not quite right.

Robin and Korree hastened back to the rear of their cave to the reclining figure of the speaker. In the light of Korree's head-stalk, it was indeed a man, an Earth man!

He was lying, tied hand and foot, on a pile of scraps, but he was raising his head, staring at them eagerly. He was a young man, evidently not much older than Robin. His blue eyes looked at them with relief and he smiled widely.

"You are a human! I thought I was dreaming when I heard a voice I could understand. You must be an American...then the Americans must have beaten us here after all!"

Robin knelt down by the man, worked at his bonds. They were tight, real cord of nylon or some Earth-made substance. It took the combined strength of the two of them to finally open the knots and free the man.

"Who are you?" Robin asked, as he worked. "Do you have a rocket on the surface?"

The man got to his feet, rubbed his muscles. He was dressed in a simple blue one-piece flyer's coverall. He was taller and slimmer than Robin, and his hair was tousled and reddish.

"My name is Piotr Ivanovitch Kareff," he said, bowing with a European gracefulness. "I regret to tell you that my rocket is indeed on the surface—but there it will stay forever. We crashed. But I am so glad to see you. You do not know how glad."

Robin shook hands. "I hate to disappoint you, but I must tell you that we are in the same predicament. I have no rocket here. I was hoping when I heard your voice that you might have one we could go back in."

The other looked confused, shook his head. "No rocket? Oh, that is too bad. Very bad."

The Glassie, who had been watching them without understanding too much of the rapid-fire quality of normal speech, suddenly said, "Have hunger much. Is food here."

He turned his back on the two men, pawed through the scraps on the cave floor, coming up with some of the provisions that Robin had packed with him.

"I'm hungry, also," said the Russian. "They have not fed me since they threw me in here. Is this stuff good to eat?"

"Try it," said Robin and the three sat down and ate. Robin sat munching and stared at the other man. The first human he had seen in almost two years. A real live man! But where did he come from? How did he get here? And how was it he was a prisoner?

For a while after they had finished, they looked at each other. The Russian spoke. "You must have a story to tell me, Robin Carew. How did you say you got here?"

Robin briefly outlined what had happened to him, the other listening attentively. When Robin had finished, he asked, "Now I want to know about you? It's your turn."

"Yes," said Piotr, "I shall tell you."

CHAPTER FOURTEEN
The Man From Lake Baikal

"I WAS an orphan of World War II," said Piotr Ivanovitch Kareff in a quiet voice, speaking precise English with a fair fluency. "My family were all vanished, I know not what happened to them. I was brought back to Russia by our soldiers and sent to a state school in the Urals set up to take care of such as myself.

"There I was a good scholar and I made myself good marks. When I was old enough, I qualified for study at a higher institute and was sent to a college for engineers. I was always interested in astronomy and rocket aviation and I was therefore trained along those lines.

"When I was eighteen, I was allowed to continue my engineering education as a part of my military duty. I was in the army, yet still studying, only this time I was stationed at one of the big experimental centers we have deep in Siberia. You probably do not know about them. They are very secret.

"The one I was at was located near the shores of Lake Baikal, the big inland sea in Central Asia near Mongolia. This was the biggest center for the study of liquid-fuel rockets. While I learned the theory, I also worked on the actual projects and helped fire many of our big rockets. These were designed after the German V-2, the same designs you Americans are also building on. We, too, had captured German scientists who had worked on these. They had much to show us, and one of the smartest of these men was the Captain Von Borck who even became a member of the party or so he said.

"I am not a political man, I am really interested in rockets, so I did not pay too much attention to these things. Von Borck may be truly believing what he desires, I do not know, but I think he is just what you call an opportunity seeker.

"After my army service, I chose to remain at the Lake Baikal station as a regular engineer. I worked on the thousand-mile rockets, and finally on the satellite rockets, and I helped get them up there. It was a nice race with you Americans. We knew a little of your plans—those you publish in the papers—and we always were urged to beat you. Sometimes we did. Sometimes you beat us.

"At our centers we made a game of this. It was serious to our country, but to us, men of science, all discoveries by human beings are great things. We liked to think of our work as a great game of mental chess with you Americans—with the pieces on the board carefully hidden from sight and reported only through guesswork and bad witnesses.

"When the satellites were up and flying their orbits around the Earth, yours and ours, the next game was obviously to race for the Moon. Should we plant the Red flag there, or you the Stars and Stripes? So we worked at that. We did not this time know what you were doing. Maybe you had different ideas.

"So Van Borck discovered a means of using atomic explosions in a steady rocket stream and explained the principle. We worked on this motor a while and finally the Ministry ordered the building of one rocket which could fly to the Moon with this super-powerful engine. At first our commander at the base said it should be a robot-piloted model, but Moscow did not want that. They wanted that men should go on that first trip. They wanted that a Soviet man should be first to reach the Moon.

"They did not know about you, Robin, and your stowaway trip! Ha! But even the Americans do not apparently know about you, alas for both of us!"

Piotr stopped a moment, got to his feet, went to the door of the cave and listened. He came back. "No one there watching us. I go on," he said.

"So finally was built a big rocket with the first atomic explosive engine. Von Borck himself was going to go in it as its engineer. But Von Borck was not really a Soviet man, and I do not think Moscow was happy about it. So they allowed for the ship to have a three-man crew. I was selected, because I am young and quick and have a good record, and also maybe because I have no family to be sorry I not come back maybe. Arkady Pavlovitch Zverin was the third, who was also an orphan.

"Came a day when the big rocket was complete and ready. We said goodbye to our friends and at the right time we went up the ladder and into our big rocket. That day, which seems to me so long ago, must have been not even a week ago yet!

"We took off perfectly, we blasted for ten minutes—I thought my head would burst—and we were on our way. Von Borck piloted it, but there was really little to do. When it came time to reverse the rockets and make our landing, we had trouble. Our gyroscope control was stuck and we had to fight with it by hand to move it. This made a delay and when we did get our jets reversed and working, our timing was off. Von Borck struggled to slow us up and come to a real stop, but we were a little too fast. We came down blasting away, and we hit very hard.

"The rocket was partly smashed. The engines and tubes all crushed. The nose was badly jarred and poor Arkady was killed by the impact. Von Borck, too, was thrown from his seat, knocked unconscious on the floor of our little cabin. I was badly bruised, but I remained conscious.

"Fortunately for us, the little cabin remained airtight. When all was still, I looked over what happened. I looked outside. We were in a large crater, whose bottom was crisscrossed with cracks. One of these, running into the distance, was quite glassy and I saw that something like steam was issuing from a point near it. This meant to me that somewhere underneath the surface there might be a place with air and water.

"I had at first thought all was lost and I would remain in the little cabin until the air was used up or the food gave out. This would be only a few days. But I thought that any chance, however little, was better than no chance. So I managed to get to the locker and get out two space suits. One I put on Von Borck who was still unconscious, but whom I could not leave behind. The other I got into myself.

"I took the German over my shoulder and managed to get out of the ship through the lock which was still intact. Carrying my companion—it was easy, he was so light on the Moon—I explored the cracks near where the ship fell. I found a way leading down and even a series of very natural air locks—a most unusual development.

"Passing through many caves and tunnels I made my way and finally got to this one. Von Borck had regained consciousness but he was not in his right senses. He was talking nonsense. He believed—I do not know how to put it—he was the King of the Trolls. He thought he was somewhere in—fairyland or hell or some supernatural place. He did not remember the trip.

"When we first met these Moon people—you call them Glassies—Von Borck said they were his Trolls. He killed four of them with his own hands and the rest became afraid of him, thought him a god or demon come to rule them. He let me alone a little while, then he seized me, tied me up himself, and put me here.

"I am afraid that he plans to sacrifice us. He is completely crazy and he has these Glassies obeying him. I am sorry for us."

Piotr stopped talking. He looked at Korree appraisingly. Robin understood his intention. "I'm afraid that Korree won't have any influence with these Glassies. They are a different tribe."

Robin rubbed his hands a bit. "I really think we should be able to escape, even so. We now outnumber Von Borck two to one and I think if we pick our time we could manage to make a getaway. We'll have to be careful. Do you think you could get back to your rocket on the surface?"

The Russian nodded. "I guess we could. I was planning to go back from the start."

"Is there anything there could use to signal the Earth with?" asked Robin. "A radio, flares, mirrors?"

Piotr nodded. "We had speaker-radio equipment, but it was smashed in the landing. It was the first thing I tried after we hit. But we do have flares. We could signal with them."

"I imagine," said Robin, "that both the Americans and Russians must be working on Moon rockets now. If we can signal back there, the next rocket along might come to this crater and find us."

"Good," said the Russian rocketeer. "Only how do we get to the surface? I have a space suit, which is probably in Von Borck's cave. Von Borck must have a suit too, if we can find it, though I think it will be much too big for you."

Robin explained about his homemade space suit. Piotr was quite impressed. The suit, which was packed in Robin's big sack, was in the prison cave where it had been thrown and they unpacked it. Piotr examined the helmet with interest. "Very good. It might work. It seems airtight."

"I tested it under water," said Robin. "It didn't leak any bubbles."

The Russian nodded. "But I don't believe your big bag of air would work. How would you blow it up in the first place? I think you would have had a hard time anyway. But fortunately there are three oxygen tanks on my own suit. I can detach one for your use."

He nodded, looking over the homemade helmet. In the half light of the cave Robin looked at his new friend with interest. There was something about his face, which struck an odd chord in Robin's mind. Something about him brought back faint, almost forgotten memories, dim frightening memories of bombs exploding, of falling buildings, of a frightened child, and great loss.

Robin suddenly asked, "How did you learn to speak English so well?"

Piotr looked up. "I was wondering when you would ask that. I always knew English, I spoke it as a little child. When I was found by the soldiers in Dresden, I was but a little boy, maybe six or seven. I spoke some German, but mostly I spoke English. They could find no sign of my parents, my family, so they took me back to Russia with them. I studied English too in school, but I always knew it."

Robin started, his heart pounding very strangely. "Where did you get your name? That's Russian."

The other stared at him hard. "No, it's not. My name—Piotr Ivanovitch Kareff—means Peter the son of John Kareff."

Robin was sure he knew now, but he doggedly insisted on his next question. "My father's name was also John. John Carew. And how do you spell your last name?"

"Why," said Peter, a curious smile beginning to force its way to his lips, "just like it's pronounced in Russia—Kareff—

C-A-R-E-W—Kareff."

And at the same instant, tears of joy sprang uncontrollably to their eyes and the two brothers grabbed each other, laughing and pounding one another's back in wild reunion.

Korree stared uncomprehendingly at the curious sight of two Earth men apparently taken leave of their senses.

CHAPTER FIFTEEN
Getaway Bomb

AFTER they had recovered from their outburst of enthusiasm the two let go of each other and sat down out of breath. "Well, this is really amazing," said Robin finally. "Here I have to go to the Moon to find my brother. You know I really do not remember very much."

"Of course not. You could not have been mere than four years old when we parted. I was about three years older, I guess. Perhaps we can put what we do know together and find out what did happen. I know that Father and Mother were interned in Germany by the Nazis. That when the war was nearing its end, the Germans started to move them and other prisoners around. In the confusion, we were stranded somewhere and there was heavy bombardment going on. I lost you and Mom and Dad somewhere, wandered by myself for many days. I was with a band of Russian people who had been taken to Germany by the Nazis to do slave labor. They were making their way back to their homes and I clung to them. So the Soviet Army simply counted me among its own orphans and took me back. But maybe you know more about our family?" Peter looked expectantly at his younger brother.

Robin nodded. "I don't remember what happened. I was too young. I only remember being terribly frightened and alone and things going bang. When I was older I looked up the orphanage records. It seems that Dad had been some sort of business agent in Germany and when the U.S. got into the war he was interned along with Mom and the two of us. Evidently they were killed in some sort of bombardment at the war's end and I was the only one who survived. You are listed as having been killed with them, according to the American Army report."

Korree was moving restlessly during this conversation, not understanding very much of it. Now he pulled at Robin's sleeve, pointed. "Look. Cheeky come."

Sure enough Robin's simian pet had finally found them. Evidently having easily avoided capture by the Glassies, the little animal had been searching for his master. Now his little head appeared around the edge of the big rock that sealed their cave. At a whistle from Robin, Cheeky pushed his way through the narrow gap and scampered to his friend.

Peter watched the monkey with interest. "I wonder if we can't make use of your pet to help us get out of here," he said. "We really ought to start thinking of escape. I don't know when Von Borck will take the notion to start something bad."

"Well, let's start planning it out," said Robin. "First, we ought to see what we have to work with. I think that the Glassies simply threw everything I had with me in here too. That should make things fairly simple. What did they have of yours?"

They went over to the pile of things, with Korree along to light the way, and examined it. Everything was present. Of Peter's property, his space suit was there, intact, with its three shoulder oxygen tanks. Robin picked up a gun belt that had evidently been part of the outfit, but the holster was empty. Peter commented, "Von Borck took it when he turned on me. He is armed also."

But Robin noticed that the German rocket pilot had evidently not thought to take the pack of additional pistol ammunition that was clipped to the belt. He withdrew a clip and turned it over, then said:

"We should be able to use these to start a diversion of some sort. If we can get their attention elsewhere, we can easily push aside the rock that seals our cave and make a run for it. We ought not to wait for Von Borck to make up his mind."

"Ah yes," said his brother. "There is good gunpowder in those bullets. We could make a small bomb for a fuse or a display."

"I think a bomb will do the trick. Let's get at it." Robin suited his action to the words. He sat down, spread a clean piece of cloth he found among Peter's property on the floor and began to pull the cartridges apart and gently shake out the powder.

Back on Earth, such a job would have been hard without instruments and great force. Here on the Moon, it was not easy but their strength enabled them to twist off the metal rims. Soon they had a neat little pile of explosive powder gathered together.

This they packed into a small glass tube among Peter's explorational equipment until it was tight and filled the space. They twisted a dry fiber until it was cord-like and rolled it in a little remaining powder till it was thoroughly blackened. This they inserted in the end of the tube as a fuse.

"Now we should get our stuff together and get ready," said Robin. "I don't think it would be a good idea to go back the way I came in; we'd just be cutting ourselves off. The idea is to reach your rocket on the surface. Which way did you come?"

Peter indicated the opposite direction. "I came in through a hole rather high in the wall, came down here along a narrow ledge. I can find it again, I think."

"Then let's get into our equipment and get ready," said Robin. He began to load his huge pack again, but Peter intervened.

"You really can leave some of that behind now," he said. "Make it easier to move fast. Besides we've got some narrow places to squeeze through on our way to the surface. I'd suggest leaving most of the food behind. Take enough for a couple of meals more. You'll only need your space helmet and space clothes."

Peter was climbing into his space suit, an airtight rubberized affair with electric heating grids. This on, he put on his space helmet for the sake of convenience, though he left the little panel of the face window open. Robin slung his own helmet from his shoulder—its vision plate, being homemade, was fixed in place.

When they were ready, they went over to the entrance and peeked through the narrow, open space. "Why, it's dark outside!" said Robin.

Where before the deep cleft had been lighted by the white light of the outside sun, now it was dark. It was not as dark as the bubble-caverns below had been, for a faint light still penetrated down from the ceiling. They could make out the darker shadows of the surrounding growth, and the Glassies outside were moving figures each illuminated by a small circle of light from their head stalks.

"Evidently the sun is going down on the Moon's surface," said Peter. "It was low on the horizon when my rocket arrived. I wonder how cold it will get in this place?"

"It seems to be a little colder already," said Robin. "This may bring Von Borck out of his cave to see what's happening."

Robin called to Korree, explained what they were about to do. Then while Korree kept a hand on Cheeky, the two Earthlings leaned their shoulders against the big boulder and pushed it aside easily—an effort, which would have blocked Moon muscles.

Korree had dimmed his headlight and the two men kneeled down and carefully lighted the fuse of their bomb with Robin's flint and steel. The end of the fiber sputtering, Robin took Cheeky and pressed the glass vial into the monkey's paws. "Over there," he whispered to the monkey urgently, and pointed a finger to the darkness opposite the direction in which they would be heading. "Take it over there and leave it," he whispered.

He'd often taught Cheeky to fetch and carry, and he hoped the animal would obey. It did. Grabbing the glass tube with its smoking fuse, the monkey dashed off into the darkness.

"I hope he remembers to drop it and come back," said Robin. Peter nodded, "Let's get started."

The men and Korree started slowly out of the cave. There was a very faint dimness about them, a starlight glow that was just enough to distinguish the presence of objects. They moved slowly, avoiding the telltale lights of passing Glassies. Korree kept his own stalk-light dark.

Suddenly the peace and darkness were split by a sharp, violent explosion somewhere behind them. Immediately following was a screeching, recognizable as the sound of an angry monkey and almost as frightening.

For an instant there was stunned silence and then pandemonium broke loose. Glassies came running in all directions, slamming into each other, not knowing what had happened. Some were running away from the noise, some were running to investigate the terrible bang, and others were simply running for cover in the caves. In the mad helter-skelter, Robin and Peter and Korree ran as fast as they could to the far end of the cleft.

They dodged tree stalks, pushed through other patches, stumbled occasionally over obstacles, but carried on. Robin noticed even as he ran that the vegetation was already drying up and dying rapidly. The cessation of sunlight had probably been quite abrupt as the sun had sunk behind whatever crater walls made up the horizon above them. Evidently the growth here was geared to a short, heavy life and sudden death.

Over the frightened, high-pitched voices of the Glassies, Robin now heard another sound, the roaring voice of a man. Von Borck had been brought out. He was yelling something, shouting angrily.

Peter called to Robin as they dashed along. "He's trying to get them to order. He knows we did it. But they don't understand him."

ONE AGAINST THE MOON

On they ran. Now behind them they heard some signs of pursuit. Evidently Peter was overoptimistic. Somehow Von Borck must have managed to get the Glassies to realize his meaning. Hitting some and shoving others, he had clearly gotten a few, who were still in awe of his "magic," to follow him. They could hear the sounds of stalks cracking far behind them as they ran. But they had a good head start.

Robin had been hanging on to Korree's arm, dragging him with him in huge, leaping steps. But as they dashed on, he realized that Peter was slowing his own steps to accommodate and that the sounds of Von Borck's rush behind them were beginning to be louder.

Korree evidently realized this too. "Leave me," he gasped. "I make out." With a twist he slipped out of Robin's hand and ran into the darkness.

"Wait!" yelled Robin after him, stopping. But Peter turned back, grabbed his brother. "He's right. He'll be better off here. We couldn't get him to the surface anyway. Come on! Quick!"

With a sudden lurch of his heart and lump in his throat Robin recognized the truth of this. He grabbed Peter's hand and the two of them started off faster than ever, heading for the far wall in huge Earthborn leaps.

It was an eerie experience dashing madly along in the near blackness of the cleft. The faint glow which came from above, probably only the light of a million million faraway stars, filtered through the curious translucent material of the cleft top, serving only to make patches of blackness against patches of even greater blackness. Far behind them a faint flickering indicated the movements of the natives. Now and then a startling flicker would prove the presence of some startled Moonworm, uncovered as a stalk was thrown over in the rush.

Behind them they could hear a crashing and every now and then a shouted word. Robin wondered what was being said, but Peter, sensing his wonder, gasped out, "He's shouting...the word for devils! When he came to...he believed himself in some sort of Troll kingdom...with me as a...devil."

"Crazy! Stark raving mad!" shouted Robin back.

On they went. The helmet banging against Robin's back made him feel clumsy and odd, yet he moved through the air with the agility of a phantom.

Now, suddenly, there loomed a dark wall before them and they caught themselves back just in time to keep from smashing headlong into it. "The wall!" shouted Robin.

Peter pulled his arm, started hurrying along to one side. He gave a sharp cry of relief, pulled Robin to him. "Here we are, the ledge. Go on up!"

Peter started off. Robin followed as fast as was possible. There was evidently a thin ledge running up the side of the cave. In places it was a gentle slope angling upward, in other parts there was a sudden step. In their haste there was no time to pick and choose their steps. Several times Robin tripped, almost falling, but he had built up such a momentum that he simply slammed and banged over the obstacles, charging up the ledge with a luck and agility that would have made a mountain goat jealous.

Behind them, at the base of the cliff, they now heard Von Borck's roaring. *"Teufel!"* he was calling. Then suddenly from where the madman stood, there beamed out a flash of yellow light. A flashlight, thought Robin, he had a flash.

The beam passed rapidly over the cave wall seeking the escapers. Once or twice they froze against the side as it passed over them, dashing on as soon as it was gone. Then Von Borck's light caught them, held them.

"Keep running," yelled Peter, "it's not far now!"

The two kept up. Then there was a sharp report below them and something went *spang* on the rock wall near Robin. A bullet…the mad rocket pilot was firing at them.

Now they simply raced on, ignoring the German's wild shots. "Here we are!" gasped Peter and seemed to melt right into the cliff face. Robin saw the black opening in the next second and tumbled into it, to be caught by his brother's arms.

For an instant they stood there in the darkness, catching their breath. Then a light appeared in Peter's hand, and Robin saw that he held an electric torch there, part of his space-suit equipment. The beam illuminated a narrow, dark tunnel leading steeply upward apparently through the solid rock.

"This way!" said Peter and started off. Robin followed him on into the narrow path that would lead him at long last to the surface of the Moon.

CHAPTER SIXTEEN
On the Crater floor

THE TUNNEL was very narrow, a mere crack in the wall, and Robin was hard put to squeeze through in a couple of spots. But it was not too long and, in a few minutes, Robin felt from the change in air and echo that it had opened out into a wider area.

Peter's flash confirmed this. They were in a small air-pocket bubble several yards wide. They crossed this while Peter searched along the floor. He stopped, pointed down.

"We go down again, through this hole in the floor. There's a short drop of only a few feet, but be careful."

Peter stepped over to the hole, sat down, and eased himself out of sight. Robin looked down, could see the floor of another cave just below. He dropped his pack through and squeezed down.

Here they were in a sort of shallow flow running lengthwise, and they had to walk in a crouched position to keep their heads from bumping the low ceiling.

Robin wondered how Peter knew which way to go, but looking carefully, he realized that his brother was only following the trail of his footsteps made on arriving—for there was a thin coating of dust on this floor that showed the trail.

"How did you ever find this passage?" asked Robin, his voice echoing flat and high in the passage.

"Saw the sealed cleft top running across the bottom of this crater. Found a spot near it where some sort of gas was hissing out. Went down it, and simply followed every lead that pointed in the direction of the cleft." Robin knew that behind this reply undoubtedly lay a lot of sweat and agony. Peter had made the trip carrying an unconscious body with him!

The low passage ended in a small cave-bubble. A break at the top of this was the next line of direction. Peter had simply dropped down on his arrival, but they waited to catch their breath. They would have to jump for it.

"Do you suppose Von Borck is following us?" asked Robin while waiting.

Peter shook his head. "I doubt it. First, we'd probably have been able to hear him coming. Second, he'd still know enough to go get his space suit before following us. Third, he won't remember anything of this trip and will have to find his way."

Rested, Robin gave Peter a boost, hoisting him as high as he could to the top of the cave-bubble. Peter jumped the short distance remaining, catching a grip on the edge of the hole in the cave ceiling. He pulled himself up, then dropped his nylon cord down for Robin to grasp and help himself up.

Up above there was still another small bubble, broken on one side. A whole series of broken bubbles lay revealed, and they walked along this section gingerly. This area was greatly cracked and seamed. It was clear to them that there was a possibility of a fall-in.

Beyond that group they came to another break leading upward, and again they moved on. Now Robin found himself breathing very heavily. "I'm getting very tired," he gasped at last.

Peter stopped. They were still in the break and a severe slope was rising before them. "It's the air pressure. It's getting quite low already. You've been used to the low pressure of the bubbles below, as you tell me, but we are close to the surface and the limited amount of air sealed in this particular bubble-system is thinning beyond the safety point. We'll have to go slow and rest often. I don't want to have to use our oxygen supplies until we are at the limit of our natural abilities."

Robin finally caught his breath, felt power returning. Now the two pushed on, going very carefully and slowly, with rests every few steps.

The steep rise ended at a narrow opening. Peter paused here, motioned to Robin to join him. "This is the crisis point," he said. "Listen."

Robin strained his ears. He was aware of the pounding of his heart struggling for oxygen. He was aware of a ringing in his ears from the low pressure. But now he heard over that a thin whistling, a high, steady rustling whistle coming from somewhere across the narrow, long cave he was looking in upon.

"What is it?" he whispered.

"A most unusual phenomenon," whispered Peter back. "The only thing that keeps the air in all this subterranean region from being sucked away to the surface. It's a volcanic current of hot gas, racing through this long channel at tremendous speed. It must come up from somewhere in the still-warm interior; it must be rushing to some vast cold spot below. But it serves as an effective curtain cutting off the stale air on this side from the near-vacuum of the surface. Its density, velocity, and heat perform the miracle."

Peter shone the lamp across and down the cave. The passage cleared a long, tunnel-like channel, which ran down into darkness on one side and away into equal darkness on the other. Only a few yards across from them he could see the gray surface of the wall. There seemed to be nothing else except the whistling noise.

"Edge along the wall here carefully," said Peter, and started off. He kept one shoulder rubbing the wall near them and walked carefully down the passage.

Robin edged out, following him closely. He felt no movement of air, yet he detected a faint trace of warmth on his outer side. Somewhere, invisible to him, that cataract of volcanic air was flowing. Was it a few feet or a fraction of an inch? He could not tell.

The wall bellied wider a little, allowing a chance to get farther away from the unseen wind. Peter was waiting here. "I think we'd better adjust our space equipment now. We have a short way to go, then we'll have to fight our way across that air blast. There's an opening to the surface at one point nearby. Once we cross the wind and get to it, we'll be outside."

Robin let down his pack. Peter examined Robin's equipment again, looking worried. He shook his head once or twice. "I hope it works out all right, but some changes will have to be made."

He took the big bladder Robin had constructed as an air bag. "This won't work, but it will come in handy in a different way." He took Robin's pocket knife and began to cut the big sack apart to make thin long strips of leather. When he had finished with that, he looked over at Robin and said:

"Now you'll have to wind these strips around you as tight as you can. Begin as high up on your chest as possible, and go on down. Wind them around your arms and legs, around your fingers, if possible. Don't undress, but wind the strips over your clothes. Make them tight. I'll help you."

As they worked to do so, Peter explained further. "Having an air helmet is not enough for space. The pressure of your blood and the gases in your system will make it impossible for you to breathe or move, if your body is not tightly encased. A real space suit like mine is pressurized, built with a layer of air pockets all over, which increase their pressure in proportion to the decrease outside. But if you don't have this pressure, even having air around your head will not help. So make those bandages tight, as tight as you can without stopping your breathing completely."

They worked on, winding the leather around and around, until Robin felt as if he were being encased in a strait jacket, felt like a living mummy. Strips were wrapped around his fingers under his gloves, his gloves fitting over them and further strapped.

Next Peter strapped one of his three oxygen tanks to Robin's back. "I hope this will work well enough to keep you breathing until we reach the rocket. Fortunately you made your helmet deep enough to come down far over your shoulders. I can work this air tube up high enough for you to grasp the end in your mouth. The air will force its way into your lungs. You'll have to struggle to force your exhalation out of your nose. It's difficult, especially the first time, but you'll have to cope with it."

As he held the helmet preparatory to putting it over Robin's head, he gave him some last-minute instructions. "We won't be able to communicate once I get this on you. You've no radio and your mouth will be full anyway. So listen carefully.

"The rocket is about a hundred yards away. I'll lead the way, and I'll tie this cord around your waist so you won't lose me. Follow me as close as you can. There's a possibility that your glass plate may fog up or ice over from the water vapor inside your helmet. If it does, hang on to the cord and keep moving after me! But don't stop…and don't give up! All set?"

Robin's heart was beating fast, he felt strange and stifled in his bindings. This was the zero instant. He nodded, held out his hand. Peter grasped it, shook it. "When you're all set, follow me across the wind stream. It's powerful—don't let it throw you."

Robin put the end of the air tube in his mouth, Peter pushed the homemade helmet down over his head, secured it tightly, almost painfully, until no space was left for air to escape. Then Peter reached behind Robin to the small tank strapped there and turned a petcock.

Instantly Robin started to choke as he felt something being rammed down his lungs. He caught himself, recognizing that his lungs were being forcibly inflated. He struggled to get control of his diaphragm to expel the excess air pressure. He managed finally to do so, feeling a whiff of air rush through his nostrils. He fought a bit more with the unpleasant current, felt himself getting a grip on it.

Through the plate of his helmet he saw Peter watching him anxiously. Then Peter rapidly tied the nylon cord around his own waist, let it out a few feet, and tied the other end around Robin's. Peter snapped shut the visor of his own helmet, touched the air controls of his own suit, and nodding to Robin, stepped out into the tunnel.

Robin followed closely, conscious of the tight, restricting bands, still fighting the unpleasant pressure of the air tube blowing down his lungs. Peter walked a few steps, pointed a gloved hand across the passage, shone his light.

There was a narrow black gap across there. Through it Robin caught a glimpse of bright white specks—the stars!

Then Peter made a dash, seemed to be picked up by a giant hand and whirled wildly across the passage. The cord tightened and Robin jumped into the space to avoid being pulled off his feet.

He was struck at once by a terrific onrush. A hot, violent blast slammed into him. He lost his footing, felt himself being hurled headlong into a furious tornado. The cord leaped out, and Peter pulled on it hard. Robin swung about, fetched up against the other side of the wall of the cave with a bang, was pulled to his feet before he had even started to fall, and was propelled right through the gap in the wall.

Suddenly all was still. The whistling of the wind, the roar of the current as it struck him, had vanished. Only the sucking and rushing of the oxygen in his own helmet could be heard. He was outside, on the surface of the Moon at last!

The gap opened from the wall of a cliff. Above him, the cliff soared to become a mountainous edge of a deep, wide crater. He turned his head, but Peter was impatient. He felt the pull of the cord, turned and followed Peter, who was moving away from the crater wall in long, low strides, strides that ate up distance like an Earthly giant in seven-league boots. Robin adjusted his pace, followed closely.

For a while he forgot his personal danger and simply gazed around at the fabulous moonscape. The crater's other wall was maybe a dozen miles away, but the thin air—the almost indetectably tenuous air that clustered at the bottom of this crater made the distance seem nothing. He could even make out details of the far edge.

And yet this section of the Moon was in the night-time. The sun had passed it by. It should have been dark, pitch-dark, by the logic of the interplanetary space. Yet it wasn't. Everything instead was bathed in a cold greenish-blue light that covered the surface like the glow of a half-dozen full moons.

He looked up. Directly in the center of the sky overhead was the source of the radiation. A great glowing ball of green and blue and white, a ball with a misty aura surrounding it, a globe that struck Robin instantly as familiar. It was the Earth. The home world, seen in all its glory, a giant full-moon Earth, continents and islands clearly outlined, a glory of pale colors, poles agleam with dazzling white…it was a sight that momentarily stopped Robin in his tracks, hypnotized with wonder.

The cord pulled him out of it, and on he dashed, looking about him in the pale Earthlight.

The surface was thick with cosmic dust, here and there the rounded dome-like surface of a congealed volcanic bubble. Cracks crossed and crisscrossed the surface, and Peter and he had to bound across many of them. He saw rising slightly above the surface a long rill of whitish substance, racing across the crater bottom. With a start he realized that that must be the glasslike roof of the great cleft he had so recently escaped from.

Above, the sky was nearly black and myriad stars shone bright from the distance. The outlines of the surrounding mountains walled in the two boys as if they were pygmy boxers in a gargantuan ring.

Robin was forcing the air from his nostrils, allowing the oxygen to rush into his lungs. He began now to feel the first faint chill of surrounding space. He realized that it must already be nearly a hundred and fifty below zero on the surface, probably even much more than that. He had to keep moving, keep moving.

But it was getting colder. He felt the cold penetrate him as his suit radiated the warmth that was in it. Now he wondered what was happening outside. Something was obscuring his view. Was it mist he was passing through?

He had heard of mist on the Moon's surface, but he had seen none when he had first emerged. Yet his vision was being obscured more and more by a cloudiness. He strained his eyes, suddenly realized that the mist was not outside, it was inside! The slight amount of vapor inside his helmet was beginning to frost up on the inside of his face plate. What Peter had feared was beginning to happen.

Robin missed his footing, stumbled, not having seen the little ridge they had passed. Peter, now barely visible ahead of him, had not stopped. Robin felt the cord tighten as he slowed down, uncertain of where his feet were landing.

He began to feel groggy, realized that he was becoming frightened. He gritted his teeth on the unpleasant air tube, said to himself, *Get a hold on, stay firm. Only a few more steps to go. Hang on! Hang on!*

He conquered his panic. Blind or not, he would keep on until he passed out. The face plate was now solid white, completely opaque. He stumbled on, allowing the tight cord to direct him, pull him.

On and on, the journey seemed endless. Running, jumping, and bouncing, his feet banging against unseen rocks, hitting into cracks, kicking out, flying through space in bounds of blind horror. It was a nightmare such as he'd never dreamed.

Then, as he came down hard and banged into something, he felt his helmet slip a little, jog slightly. There was a *whish* and suddenly his face plate cleared completely. At the same instant he felt as if his eyes would pop, while something snatched at his nose and sucked the breath from him.

Through the clear plate he caught a wild glimpse of a large metallic structure sticking up out of the ground. The Russian rocket, he thought wildly. It was big like a huge bullet, gleaming brightly and polished. He saw it nearing him, realized he was being dragged along by Peter.

He realized also that his helmet had slipped a gap, so that the air within had been sucked out, that the water vapor clogging his face plate had been snatched out with it, and that his face was exposed. But the oxygen tube was still in his mouth, still forcing air into him, and his nostrils were having it sucked out almost as fast. Somehow the thin stream of air rushing from the helmet kept his face from all the rigors of vacuum. His eyes were bulging and paining, he felt his nose spraying blood and a red film kept clogging the face plate and being snatched away by the escaping air.

Then as he realized he could no longer stand the agony, he felt himself grabbed under the shoulders, hoisted up, shoved into a small dark space and felt through his fingers the clang of a metal door. There came a hissing noise, and as consciousness at last oozed away from him, he knew that they had reached the air lock of the Soviet rocket and that his ordeal was over.

CHAPTER SEVENTEEN
Moon Calling Earth

THE IMPRESSION of a damp cloth moving gently over his face was Robin's first sensation on recovering his senses. He opened his eyes to find Peter leaning over him, carefully mopping away the soreness from his nose and face. Robin's eyes hurt and he blinked several times, each time feeling their rawness.

"Easy does it," said Peter, smiling. "Your eyes are very bloodshot, but fortunately there's no real damage. You couldn't have been exposed to the outside for more than a few seconds. Nosebleed's stopped, too."

Robin raised his head, feeling a little dizzy and weak at first. He was lying in a hammock slung across the narrow space of the rocket's tiny cabin. He took in the limited quarters slowly, while flexing his muscles to discover other points of sensitivity. His clothing had been removed, the tight bandaging unwrapped. He was wearing some sort of loose aviation coverall that his brother had dressed him in.

"Have I been out long?" Robin asked, rising to a sitting position.

"Maybe a half-hour," said his brother. "Mostly shock and overexertion, I guess. You've got some bruises on your shins and feet, but nothing that should stop you. Feel like some hot food? Real Earth food?"

Robin was suddenly hungry and the memories of a hundred forgotten foods flooded his senses. He nodded, and greedily attacked the full mess kit that his brother had been heating. It contained merely some sort of frankfurter, some canned potato, a chunk of black bread, and a cup of something that must have been condensed cabbage soup...but to Robin it was the best banquet he'd had in many months. For the first time he ate meat that wasn't rabbit or a Moon creature, vegetable that wasn't Moontree fruit. His tongue reveled in the flavors. A glass of hot tea was the final sensation.

Refreshed, he looked around. The little cabin, occupying the entire nose of the rocket, must have been a tight squeeze indeed for a three-man crew. The controls and the pilot's seat occupied a good section of it. There was space for only two hammocks, which were obviously not to be spread out except when taking off or sleeping, and Peter was rolling up the one in which Robin had been resting. There was a built-in electric grid, a nozzle from which water was piped, a large number of observational and recording instruments, a couple of folding seats, nothing much else. Several thick glass bull's-eye windows were set in a circle around the nose, at a level with the pilot's eyes. Light came from one large electric bulb hanging in the nose of the ship. The whole cabin was tilted over at an angle, the result of the crash.

"I'm surprised that everything is in such good condition," said Robin. "I had expected to see a complete ruin."

"Well," said Peter, "I've got to admit that Von Borck was definitely a good pilot. The crash was probably not his fault. We were actually not supposed to land. Our orders were to try to circle the Moon in a narrow orbit, then return. We were to land only if Von Borck was sure he could do it and get away again.

"What happened though was that after we had crossed the dividing line in space where the Moon's pull equaled the Earth's pull, our gyroscopic controls jammed. Von Borck couldn't turn the rockets in our rear to the indicated direction. We struggled with the gyro for about forty minutes, even going outside to get at the airless tube section beneath this sealed cabin. When we finally got the controls operating, it was far too late to attempt to establish an orbit. Instead, Von Borck did the next best thing—he decided to attempt a direct landing. He reversed the rocket entirely, slowed us down and came down in an effort to land on his jets. It's a very difficult balancing trick, especially on an unknown landing field with uncertain distances.

"Actually he almost succeeded. He came down just a little too fast, smashed up our tubes, rammed the whole rear down into the pumice-and-dust surface, leaving our nose cabin sticking out unharmed. Von Borck slammed his head against the metal paneling. I took a spill, and Arkady who had volunteered to stand at the opposite observation port from the pilot in order to inform him of any dangers from that side was thrown across the room and killed."

Robin nodded slowly. "But why didn't you just stay here instead of going out?"

Peter went to a wall cabin, opened it. Inside there were about a half-dozen small containers and cans. "That's the whole stock of food we have left," was the reply. "We couldn't have stayed here too long. When I looked around outside I saw mist issuing from that spot in the cliff we came through. Obviously we'd die if we didn't find some place to stay. I went outside, buried Arkady, explored a little, realized that that rill out there was a sealed cleft, which probably held air. So I loaded Von Borck, who had been unconscious for hours, and set out to go underground."

Robin got up, walked around. He was already in better shape. He looked at the panels, found them complex and with the markings in Russian. "What's the source of the electricity?" he asked.

"There's an atomic pile somewhere in the rear of the rocket," Peter replied. "That's something you don't smash easily. It's still operating."

"Can we send a message back to Earth then?" asked Robin. "If we've the power, and this ship must have a radio…"

"We tried that, but the radio was smashed in the landing. However, there is an emergency wave sender, which was designed for just such a thing. I don't know if that's working. Let's see."

Peter opened a door set in the floor of the rocket, which opened on an area jammed with equipment, wiring, and extra supplies. He reached around, extracted a small black box. He held it up, shook it gently. Handing it to Robin, he took out a roll of wire, and seating himself at the pilot's seat began to connect the box to the rocket. When it was plugged in to the electric system of the cabin, Peter flicked a switch and turned a knob. A thin humming came from the box.

"It works," he said. "This gives off a steady signal wave going on the general air-travel band. The radio buzz can be heard from Earth if it's being sought. By following it, astronomers can trace exactly where this rocket is. All we have to do is leave this on—it will run for years on our atomic power source. Eventually, rockets will locate us."

"But surely there must be some way of calling their attention even sooner?" said Robin. "Do you have flares?"

"You're right," Peter said excitedly. "We've got them. And it is night outside. If we use our flares, they could be seen on any decent-sized telescope. Shall we set them off?"

Robin nodded. "No time like now."

Peter reached again into the floor storages, opening another section, and began to pull out another space suit. "This was Arkady's," he said. "It should fit you."

It did. This time, Robin felt none of the uneasiness that had assailed him on his previous experience on the outside. In a few minutes, he and Peter were standing a short distance away from the rocket and setting out the flares.

Although the suit was cumbersome, it was not too uncomfortable. Instead of tight bandaging, the fabric of the suit consisted of some sort of self-inflating air sacs, which maintained an equal and natural pressure on the surface of Robin's body. The helmet, which was really airtight and warmed, was entirely comfortable, although again the breathing was a matter of a forced intake and a willful exhalation.

They set up the flares, which were magnesium-burning giant candles, a safe distance from the rocket, wired them to a detonator powered from the ship. Then, before going back, Robin and Peter simply stood and looked around.

All about, the giant bare mountains ringed the crater. Their gaunt, jagged outlines were a black ring against, which was set the star-strewn wonder of the sky, in whose exact center slowly rotated the marvelous globe of Mother Earth.

The eerie Earthlight threw odd shadows and dark spots across the grayness of the plain. Here and there the mysterious-looking domes rose, the tops of bubbles as Robin had reason to know. In other places smaller craters and ringed ridges broke the surface.

"It looks desolate and barren," commented Peter on the helmet-radio. "Yet, you know, when we landed in the sunlight of the Moon's day, it wasn't all like this. There were patches of low scrubby plants growing in the lowest sections near spots where some air must have been seeping out. This crater is considerably lower than much of the surrounding areas on this central part of the Moon. The air here may be almost unnoticeable, but it is still just a bit denser even than it must be on the 'seas' beyond these crater walls."

"How did you spot that break in the wall we came through?" asked Robin, turning to search for it.

"As a matter of fact, it was quite obvious," said his brother. "In the sunlight, there's a distinct stream of vapor coming out of it and a lot of frozen water vapor all around. Further, it was just there that the green vegetation was growing thickest. It was quite inviting to a man looking for refuge…otherwise I'd probably never have thought of it."

They trudged back to the rocket, climbed through the lock into the safety of the tiny cabin. Robin set the firing pin of the detonator switch, looked out. "It's the Western Hemisphere that's facing the Moon now," he said. "Just coming into view. Must be early morning around the New Mexico belt. You know, your Russian friends won't see this flare."

Peter looked up, shrugged. "We can fire another flare twelve hours later," he said. "I am not particular who rescues us. I am an American, you know. I owe something to the Soviets too. When you look at the world from here, from another planet, these distinctions of nationality seem so—somehow—unimportant. We are all humans, all from the same ancestors. Even if we were not brothers, we would feel ourselves such. Our roots go to all parts of the world. If you add up all people's ancestors a hundred generations back, you will realize that there can't be anyone who is not distantly related to everyone else—that we all share somebody in our ancestry who lived in every country of the world, shared all the histories of the past and all the different politics and opinions."

Peter grew quiet, as if a little amazed at his own outburst. Robin drew close to him, threw an arm around him. "I think when more men get out among the stars, people are going to realize that we can't afford to think of ourselves as anything other than citizens of Mother Earth. In the face of the universe, of Moonmen, of the inhabitants of the millions of other planets that must exist, our national differences seem so small, so much a private family matter as not to be thrashed out in the public of our interstellar neighbors. I think it's good we are brothers. All men are brothers."

Robin threw the switch.

Outside, the crater suddenly lighted up in a blinding white glare, a blaze that threw wild, dancing black shadows several miles across the floor, that momentarily lighted the great crags and precipices of the mountains that made an outburst of grandeur in a moonscape of unearthly terror and beauty.

Five minutes later, when the flares had died down, Robin again threw the switch. The second set of magnesium bombs went off and again the crater was brilliantly lighted.

"On Earth that should stand out very sharply. It is nearly a new moon for them. This spot of light will be like a blinding diamond on a black velvet setting," said Peter poetically.

They rested now, taking their space suits off, lolling around on two hammocks, just talking, renewing acquaintance, exchanging experiences. They ate another meal, slept, finally donned their outfits again and set off the next set of flares a half Earth-day later, when the massive area of Eurasia was on the face of the globe in the Lunar sky.

"Now the Russian observers have had a chance to see us," said Peter. "We ought to go back to the underground world again. Our supplies here are not enough. In order to eat and breathe the next few months, we will have to live among the Glassies. We have to go back to the great cleft again."

"Yes," said Robin. "And that brings up the question of Von Borck. He'll be waiting for us, you know."

His brother nodded. "Ah, but this time we will be the ones who are armed and ready." He reached down, took out a second gun belt, handed it to Robin. "Use this. Strap it around your space suit."

Robin looked at it, lifted the pistol in its holster. "It's an army automatic," said Peter. "A Tokarev .30, built much the same as an American Colt. Here, I'll show you how it works."

He cautioned about the lack of a safety catch, showed how to load the clip of bullets. "Be careful of it, though. It has a strong kickback on Earth—here on the Moon, it may be quite tricky to fire a gun."

They dressed again in their outfits, loaded on other supplies that might come in handy, including a light carbine, hunting knife and axe, and waterproof pack of matches. They slung the gun belts around their waists, tied the nylon cord to each other as an added precaution, and made a last check of the rocket cabin.

The little radio signal was still humming. Some day it would bring a rescue ship. Whether that would be a matter of months or a matter of years was the only question. Robin gulped a bit at the prospect of spending more years away from his own world. Sight of Earth, the taste of real food had made him quite homesick.

He thrust such thoughts away, snapped tight his helmet plate, and nodded to Peter. They climbed out of the rocket, sealing the air-lock door. They stood for a moment outside the wreck, taking their bearings.

They turned to head for the cliff wall, when something went *ping* off a metal fixture on Robin's helmet.

He started, pulled back and something seemed to flick past his eyes and pop against the side of the rocket.

He yelled and ducked for cover. "Look out, Peter! Get down!"

Standing on the surface, just outside the narrow crack that led underground, was the figure of a man—a man wearing a space suit similar to theirs, with a small dark object in his hand which issued a little flash of red fire.

"It's Von Borck," gasped Robin, "and he's shooting at us!"

CHAPTER EIGHTEEN
Madman's Battle

ROBIN lay flat against the ground, holding himself motionless. Peter's voice came over his helmet-radio. "Did you get hit?"

"No," said Robin. "Something may have chipped my helmet but there's no leak, so I guess it wasn't a direct shot. How about you? Where are you?"

From his position he couldn't see his brother, who had obviously fallen somewhere near. "I'm down just behind you," came Peter's voice. "We'll have to find better cover than this. There's a slight ridge about a foot high a, couple of yards to your left. Crawl over to it and get behind it."

Robin cautiously raised his head. It drew no fire and he realized that lying down in the darkness of the gray surface, the greenish Earthlight was not sufficient to outline him to Von Borck's eyes. He eased up on his arms and crawled slowly to the ridge. Behind this was a measure of protection. He was now free to twist his body around to look for Peter. In the cumbersome helmet and suit, the only way he could look around was to move his whole body.

Peter was crawling after him slowly. There was a sudden spurt of dust from the ground just behind him, like a tiny geyser. "Von's still shooting at you," said Robin. "Hurry!"

Peter slid quickly into refuge behind the ridge at Robin's side. Twisting his body, he unstrapped the light carbine rifle from his back, brought it around in front of him. "Have you ever fired a rifle or a pistol, Robin?" he asked.

"I learned some target shooting at school," said Robin. "I was a pretty fair shot. But I never handled a revolver."

Peter slid the rifle over to him. "Then you use this. I'll use my pistol. We'll have to get him before he gets us."

Robin held the rifle awkwardly. He glanced at it, saw that it was loaded, slid the bolt action. "I don't like this," he said. "If there was only some way we could capture him and hold him until we're rescued. You said he's a good man with rockets. Maybe he can be straightened out mentally if we can get him back to Earth."

Pete shrugged, grunted. "Don't waste time dreaming. Sure he was a good engineer. But right now it's him or us. If he has his way, none of us will ever return to Earth alive. Just remember he's doing his very best to kill us—we cannot dare do any less. Sure, if we get a break, we'll capture him. Right now, though, we'd better shoot him or we'll never get out of this alive."

Peter suited his action to his words. He clumsily forced his thickly gloved finger through the trigger guard and grasped the pistol. He swiftly raised up, aimed, and pulled the trigger.

There was a flash of red and simultaneously Peter fell over backward and rolled over once with a yell of pain. Robin turned, stricken with horror. "What happened! Are you hit?"

Peter's voice came back. "No, I'm not hit, but I almost wrenched my arm off! It was the gun's recoil, the kick! I completely forgot what a terribly strong recoil a pistol would have on the Moon. It was like holding a rocket engine in my hand for a split second. It simply hurled me right over."

Peter rolled himself over on his chest, resuming his position next to Robin. "We'll have to be careful when we fire. Remember the kick will be many times stronger than back on Earth."

There was another spurt of dust to one side of them. Another evidence of Von Borck's shooting. Possibly he had caught a glimpse of Peter's scramble.

Robin slid the rifle out in front of him, cocked it for firing. He crawled to a break in the ridge, propped the butt of the gun against a small outcropping of rock along the surface, rolled himself clumsily into position. Raising his head, he saw the figure of Von Borck still standing against the narrow entrance to the wall. He aimed the rifle as well as he was able under the handicaps, pressed it hard, and pulled the trigger.

He felt a sharp shock as the rifle tried to kick out of his hands, but he had bolstered it well. He saw a chunk of rock split from the cliffside just over the German's head. Von Borck ducked as the dust began to fall upon him in its slow Lunar fashion, then the German moved back into the break.

Robin again aimed the rifle, this time directly at the dark center of the break in the cliff. Again he fired. This time the figure of the space-suited man backed out of sight entirely.

"What now?" asked Robin. "Shall we wait for him to come back or shall we try to follow him?"

"Better take the chance and go after him," said his brother's voice. "Must follow up every advantage."

"Then let's go," said Robin and leaped to his feet. Peter jumped up with him and they both started to sprint for the entrance in the cliff.

They ran for it in low, swift leaps, and this time Robin saw what ease and fun running on the Moon's surface could be if you had the proper outfit for it. It was so light and easy, like running in a dream, gliding rapidly over the faintly lighted eerie moonscape in a world of absolute silence and motionlessness.

For an instant, as they closed in on the cliff, Robin saw Von Borck's figure appear, there was another flash of red and then the man vanished again. But the boys did not halt. Together they charged the entrance. In a matter of seconds, they reached it, blocked it.

There was no sign of the German. They shone their flashlamps into the channel behind the opening. There was nothing.

Robin could feel the faint rustling movement of the rushing air current, but he could see nothing in motion. Again he was struck by the weirdness of the phenomenon.

"Where'd he go?" he whispered, even though his voice could not be heard outside of their helmets.

"He's probably hiding somewhere. We'll have to follow him. Get ready and then remember to throw yourself hard across that air blast. It's strong." Peter checked the nylon that tied them together. "Shall I untie this or shall we jump together?"

"Let's go together," said Robin. They held hands, and, backing up, took a running start and threw themselves into the darkness of the break.

There was again the buffeting of a powerful wind, and Robin felt himself being caught off his feet by the force of a hurricane. Before he could be swept away, a jerk at the cord around his waist threw him down, and he rolled over on the windless far side of the tunnel, safe with Peter.

He became aware of outside noises. He followed Peter's example and opened the plate of his helmet. For an instant he gasped for air, then adjusted to the thin atmosphere.

Both brothers listened. But they heard nothing. "He must have headed back for the cleft," said Peter. "We'll have to follow him."

They started to retrace their tracks. Partly down the wind tunnel they found the downward slope on which they had traveled before. Robin flashed his lamp down its steep pitch. He saw nothing. Gingerly he began to work his way cautiously down the sharp slope.

Peter followed behind. Halfway down, Robin stopped for breath. When he caught it, he whispered. "I just thought of something. How do we know Von went down here? Maybe he's gone farther up the tunnel, waiting to slip back and get behind us."

"I don't think so," said Peter. "I looked in the dust up along the tunnel for his footprints and saw none. He must be ahead of us."

They slid on down the slope, found themselves at the beginning of the upper series of connected broken bubbles. Along this they trekked, passing along the debris-strewn floor, picking their way carefully. Shining their lamps ahead as they went, they saw no sign of motion.

Finally they came to the hole in the floor, through which they would have to drop several feet into the cave below. Robin switched off his light as they approached it, whispered to Peter to do the same.

They stood silently in the pitch darkness. Then Robin nudged Peter, pointed with his hand against Peter's. The hole in the floor was faintly visible. There was a dim flickering coming from it. Robin whispered, "It must be Von's flashlamp. He's down there, waiting for us."

Peter nodded in the darkness. "It was the logical spot. He probably hopes to shoot us as we drop through the hole."

The two stepped carefully up to the hole, not yet using their lights. They kneeled down, looked.

The cave below was almost dark. But from just outside it, from the tunnel that led into it, was a flickering light. Their crazed enemy was lurking there, waiting.

"What do we do now?" muttered Peter.

Robin looked carefully. "I think I have it. Untie the cord and give it to me."

Peter untied his end of the nylon rope that linked them. Robin undid his end, took his flashlamp, tied it to the cord. He whispered his plan to Peter.

Robin lit the flash, backed away from the hole several feet, and then kicked some rocks and began to make a clattering noise. At the same time he began to talk loudly, as if conversing with Peter.

Meanwhile, Peter was crouched at the edge of the hole, his Tokarev automatic firmly wedged against one side of the hole while it was pointing directly at the faint spot of light below which Von Borck was hiding.

Robin reached the hole, making sure he was creating enough noise for the rocket pilot to hear him. Then he waved his lamp a few times, flickering it around the cave below, and kneeling down, began to lower it on the cord, trying to keep its beam pointed at the tunnel in which their foe waited. This was the bait on their trap.

Just as he had expected, as the swinging lamp was about halfway down, dangling presumably in the helpless hand of a man being lowered to the floor—as Von Borck was supposed to think—the figure of the German appeared in the cave, uttering a wild yell of triumph and aiming a big pistol at the moving light.

Two guns went off at the same instant. There were two flashes of fire, two deafening blasts of sound. Von Borck's bullet shattered the swinging flashlamp, blew it into a dozen fragments.

Peter's bullet struck Von Borck in the chest, hurling him against the wall to fall in a heap on the floor.

Without wasting time, Peter simply stepped into the hole and drifted downward in the low force of Moon gravity. Robin followed suit. They leaned over the German's body.

Robin looked at the pale, mustached face, the staring eyes. "I think he's dead," he said. "Though he could be only unconscious." He reached over, started to feel the man's face to find out whether he still breathed.

"Look out!" shouted Peter suddenly and grabbed Robin, pulling him to one side. Robin looked up and back.

Above him, with maddening leisureliness, the entire ceiling of the underground bubble was dropping down, dropping in several giant chunks, several Earth tons of rock falling toward them.

With a mad scramble the two leaped to safety in the tunnel leading downward. There was a slow grinding crash as the shattered roof of the cave settled to the floor, crushing the body beneath it, blocking and sealing the tunnel.

"Come on!" Peter grabbed Robin's arm. "The rest of it is caving in! We'd better run!"

They dashed down the tunnel, as it crashed behind them. On they ran, following the twisted trail through fault and cleft and bubble, with disaster following their steps. Finally the ruin and destruction came to an end as they reached the last steep slope downward to the great sealed cleft.

"What happened?" asked Robin, as they paused at last to catch their breath.

"The explosions!" gasped Peter. "The concussions of our pistols shattered the delicate balance of the honeycomb undersurface here. We're lucky it didn't all come down at once, rather than in the form of a chain reaction. We're lucky to be alive, believe me!"

"Yes," said Robin, beginning to make his way down the last tunnel that led to the open ledge of the great bubble-world where the Glassies lived. "Yes, we're lucky to be alive, but how will we ever get back to the surface now? We're sealed in. Maybe forever."

Peter was silent as they reached the ledge, looked into the vastness of the cleft-world, saw the faint flickering lights of Moonworm and Moonman. "Maybe we'll never get out. Robinson Crusoe lived twenty-eight years on his island before he was rescued. It may be fifty before they find us in here."

Robin shrugged. "When I first landed here, I said to myself that while there's life there's hope. Now there are two of us. And that's an advance…"

CHAPTER NINETEEN
Riding the Tornado

THEY looked down from their point on the high ledge into the length of the cleft-world. A very faint light streak could be seen looking upward—this was the curious volcanic glass of the surface roof. Through it penetrated just a hint of the full Earthlight that bathed the outer moonscape. Down were shadows and darkness, in the distance little bits of moving lights, flickering sparks, that may have been the Glassies' head-stalks.

The two men used their remaining flashlamp to light up the narrow ledge. Carefully they made their way down the steep side of the cavern wall, their light swinging slowly back and forth. "Suppose the Glassies see the light?" said Peter. "We may be in for trouble."

"Maybe," said Robin, "but this time we'll be alert for it. We'll have to steer clear of overhanging spots, keep our light swinging about, but I have an idea we'll have no trouble. That bomb and the shooting will probably make them keep their distance."

Down they went until they reached the level surface. Then they started off across the space to the faraway place where the lights could be seen. It was the winter half-month now for the sub lunar world. The Moon growths had fallen, shriveled, died. Their seeds lay dormant for the next sun period. It was fairly chilly in the cavern, yet not as cold as it might have been.

Somewhere, thought Robin, there is a warm volcanic current keeping this cavern from freezing over.

They kept a good distance between each other, the long, thin, strong cord linking them being kept almost taut. The reasoning behind this was that if another lassoing attempt were made, it would be almost impossible to get both at once. As long as one were free to get at his firearms, they could overcome such an attack.

On they went, with still no sign of meeting any opposition. Then Robin saw a sudden faint flicker in a clump of darkness to one side. He stopped, whispered into his helmet-radio what he had seen. Rapidly his eyes swept the scene, and, yes, there was another suddenly doused flicker on the other side. The Glassies must be watching them, waiting.

Now the two proceeded at a slow pace, widely swinging their light from side to side to prevent ambush. "Somehow," said Robin, "we are going to have to prove we're friendly. We may have to live here a long time."

"Yes," said Peter, "but how?"

They walked only a few steps farther before the answer was given them. Something was standing directly in their path. As their light swung near it, this figure raised two hands high and its head-stalk light flashed into brilliant prominence.

It was a Glassie standing there, a transparent-bodied Moonman whose odd face bore the equivalent of a broad smile and whose chest was decorated with a painted black circle. Robin stared at the figure of this chief a moment. He saw something move on the Glassie's shoulder—a tiny, dark, manlike creature no bigger than a doll.

This creature opened its mouth, uttered a sharp shriek. "Cheeky!" gasped Robin. And at the sound of his voice the little monkey leaped from the Glassie's shoulder in one monstrous Lunar bound and arrived at Robin's foot. Another jump and it was in Robin's arms, screeching with joy.

The Glassie chief came forward. It spoke, "Robin! Good see you. Good see you." It was Korree! Now he too moved forward to grasp Robin awkwardly but happily...Korree wearing the marking of the tribal head!

Now other Glassies appeared around them, but they held no weapons in their hands, no sticky hoops or bindings. They stood around the newcomers with awe and uncertainty—willing to be guided by Korree's actions but aware of the possible results of an encounter with space-suited Earthlings.

Korree turned a moment, waved them on, speaking in their tongue. Peter came up, nodding, shoving his pistol back into its holster.

"I see your two friends have won the day while we were up above," he said. "They were indeed friends."

The two brothers were escorted back to the site of the native settlement in a crowd of bobbing head-stalk lights and jabbering Glassies. Korree explained as they walked.

It seemed that the explosion of the homemade bomb had completely disrupted the fear in which Von Borck had held the Glassies. This was greater magic to them, and it was the mysterious little being—Cheeky—who had accomplished it. In the first excitement, the Glassies had fled and hid. That was when the German had come after Peter and Robin, leaving the Glassies behind.

This, too, was an indication that even the powerful stranger who had usurped the role of chief by the expedient of his mere existence and strength had bowed to the power of the little monkey. In Moonman tribes, the chief never fled the scene of his authority. To do so was to abdicate it. Von Borck had unknowingly destroyed his authority by his abrupt chase after Robin and Peter.

When Korree made his way back to the cave-village after giving up his attempt to follow his Earthling friends, he had arrived to find the Glassies cowering in fear of the capering Cheeky, who was unhurt by the blast.

Korree had gathered up Cheeky in his arms and by so doing had made himself the master of the situation. That was how it came about that the two brothers had been met by a friendly admiring reception rather than a hostile one.

"But what happened when Von Borck returned here to get his space suit?" asked Robin.

Korree waved a hand as if the answer was obvious. "Glassies hide," he said simply. "Korree hide. Cheeky hide. Everyone hide." And so Von Borck arrived to find himself deserted and unwelcome. And he had promptly left to follow the trail to the surface.

Once back at the site of the caves, they found themselves honored guests. In the days that followed, they set up a cave for themselves, organized a home. Cheeky seemed to have now attached himself to Korree and went everywhere with the Glassie. Robin and Peter rested, set up a regimen of native food, observed the Glassies' way of life. The sun came up again on the surface and flooded the cleft with its light. The

Moontrees grew rapidly in dense profusion. The two brothers gradually explored the length and breadth of the little world, systematically working around it in search of some new path upward.

But their search seemed fruitless. There were a number of holes and breaks in the walls and caves, but none promised a place of exit to the surface.

They went back to the original ledge and tunnel, tried to work their way in, but it was blocked with fallen stone and jammed too tightly for passage.

They discussed the possibility of making explosives, blasting through, but discarded this as they realized the basic fragility of the whole cleft setup. Such blastings might do worse damage, might even crack a direct opening to the surface through which the air within the cleft-bubble would rush out, leaving it a sterile, cold, and dead region.

Finally after another Lunar night and another Lunar day, exhausting still one more Earth month, they settled down to a slow steady picking and shoveling. They worked in the blocked tunnel in all their spare time, carefully picking away chips of rock, pushing others aside, burrowing around fallen slabs, slowly, gradually, painfully working their way along the old path. But it was hard and unrewarding work. It went slowly and they were always afraid of a cave-in.

Two or three times such an event did occur, and had it not been for the slowness with which things fell on the Moon, one or the other brother would surely have been pinned down. On the third such disaster, the two quit the task, returned to their home in the Glassie village discouraged.

"This will not work," said Robin. "We'll have to give up this entire approach. It would be months or even years before we could make our entire way and by that time one of us would surely be killed in the tunnels. They are still highly unsettled, still shifting."

They sat down, looked at each other. "There must still be a way," said Peter. "We must find a way to reach the surface. Otherwise we will remain here forever."

Robin nodded, deep in thought. Another night was coming over the cleft. The sun was passing swiftly from overhead. A chill began to touch the air, as darkness blacked out the cavern. It would be another two weeks before they could resume any work on their problem. Robin started to build a fire in their cave, one they burned every Moon winter's night. As he did so a thought struck him.

He turned. "When we were first returning from the surface it occurred to me as we came out that there had to be some sort of volcanic current warming this cavern, sun or no sun. Now it seems to me that if we could find that current, we would find some sort of air stream or water stream that must go upward. We ought to look for the warmest spot in the cavern, trace it."

Peter turned, a sharp light in his eye. "And now that you say it, do you know what that current is? It's the one that passes the break in the crater wall—the constant hurricane that we broke through to get in here, which rushes by the break so hard and so fast that it seals this cavern's quiet inner air as perfectly as if it were an air lock. It has to be that very current which passes somewhere lower down and warms this cleft!"

Robin nodded, a sharp excitement stirring him. "I think we have hit on it. The night time is the time to hunt for it. Find the spot or places in this cleft that stay warmest and they must be nearest the underground wind tunnel."

So they set out on a new course of exploration, this time scouting the bubble in the dark of the night. It grew chillier, but in their space suits, which they had resumed for this expedition, they could keep warm. They found several areas along the ground where it seemed a bit warmer than in the cave generally, but after several days of search, this clue also seemed fruitless. The areas were such that no amount of digging short of high explosives would suffice.

Finally when the long Lunar night was almost over, they awakened from sleep in the cave to face the thought that this too was a blind alley. Korree entered, the monkey on his shoulder. He made his way to them, noticed their air of sadness, asked them why.

Tired, Robin explained to him what they were looking for. His Glassie friend cocked his head. "You come my home. I show you hot spot," he said.

The two men looked up. "What?" asked Peter. Korree repeated his statement. Peter looked at Robin quizzically. Without another word the two got up and followed the Glassie.

The deep cave where the chief made his home was only a short distance from their own. Here, at the very back of the chief's home, they found what they sought. There was a thin, sharp crack in the rear wall. The stone around it was definitely warmer than that in the rest of the cave. Putting their ears to the crack, they could hear the faint high whistling of the air current that must be roaring past only a foot or two beyond.

"This is why it was picked as the chief's cave," said Robin. "It's practically air-conditioned!"

The next day, after the sun had finally made its appearance, the two started to work in the back of Korree's cave. They worked carefully with axe and pick, enlarging the crack, chipping away at it. Finally, they dislodged a sizable segment of rock, enough to allow one man to squeeze through.

Sure enough, there was a dark underground channel through whose center rushed the eternal current of hot volcanic air. This channel probably had its source somewhere in the still-mysterious depths of the Moon's core. It wound and forced its way upward doubtless to dissipate somewhere, as the cold of the surface bore away its warmth, probably to wind up downward again as a mass of cold gas.

There was barely enough room at the side of the tunnel for a man to stand flat against the wall, without touching the blast.

Robin, who had gone through to examine it, came back out into the light of Korree's cave. "Well," he asked Peter, "what do we do now?"

His brother nodded. "I think we can get to the surface all right. Just get in the blast and let ourselves be blown along upward. When we find that break, we'll get out of the current and we'll be able to reach our rocket."

"Uh huh," said Robin, "and then how do we get back down here again?"

Peter shrugged. "I don't know. There must be a way."

The two returned to their own place and talked it over. But the opportunity was too good to pass up. "Sooner or later," said Robin, "we're going to do it. So we may as well face that. As for getting back, perhaps we could simply walk all the way down the channel, keeping carefully to the side of dead air just beyond the blast."

Peter frowned. "I don't think you'll find much of that. There can't be many places where such a dead air channel exists. On the other hand, if we attack the problem of returning by the old route, we may be able to find a way through it from that end—or make a new one. Back at the rocket there are explosives, better tools than those we have. I think we should risk it."

"Yes," Robin added, "I think so too. Besides, we ought to fire off some more flares. Our signals may never have been seen."

That being settled, the two Earthlings again donned their space suits, equipped themselves, tied themselves together with a length of cord. They returned to Korree's cave, explained their project and gravely shook hands with their Glassie friend.

Then Robin carefully eased himself through the break into the dark channel. Peter squeezed through after him, as Robin flattened himself along the wall and moved aside. Their helmets sealed, Robin counted to three, and then both leaped forward.

Instantly the racing wind current caught them up, snatched them off their feet. They found themselves being blown madly along the darkness like leaves before a gale.

The air was hot and Robin felt himself almost scorched as he was hurled along, his elbows and legs occasionally scraping the wall, once feeling himself somersaulting upward, twisting and turning in the horrible blast.

For a dreadful moment he felt panicky, out of control, utterly helpless in the grip of the underground tornado. He lighted the flash, saw it wildly flickering. He drew his legs up, ducked his head, and found he could get his equilibrium. Ahead of him the tunnel was ascending. He felt himself rising, felt the slight drag occasionally at his belt as Peter's bouncing body followed his.

Now the air began to cool and seemed to slow down slightly. The passage leveled off, he was whirling down a straight passage, and suddenly, in a split second of awareness, he saw a faint spot of bright light ahead of him. He rushed toward it, like a ball buoyed on a stream from a fire hose. It must be the exit to the surface, he thought, and in a second held out the axe he gripped in his hand.

The handle caught at the opening as he went sailing by, jammed, swung his body against the wall with a smack. Peter's body flashed past, caught up short by the cord, and also hit the body of airless space on the outer side of the channel.

They climbed dazedly to their feet and struggled to the narrow break. They staggered out onto the surface, now bathed in the blindingly brilliant light of the sun rising over the peaks of the farther mountains ringing the crater.

Around them were the first shoots of the stubborn and hardy surface vegetation in this crater, dwarfed cousins of the plants below.

They caught their breath. "Better get moving," said Peter finally. "This sun is dangerous."

They started across the floor of the crater, the several hundred feet to where the nose of the wrecked Russian rocket rested. Both men knew they were bruised from the short, mad trip. There would be scraped shins and knees and elbows. But they had made it, that was the thing.

They were about a hundred feet out, when suddenly Robin stopped, stared into the sky. Peter followed his glance.

There was something up there. When they had first glanced up, there was the Earth still in its place, though now but a crescent. There were the myriad stars, and the corona-encircled sun. And now there was another celestial object. A tiny spot of reddish orange was growing in the sky, growing as they watched it.

"What is it?" asked Robin in a half whisper, afraid to venture the thought that was rioting around in his head.

Peter simply stared, transfixed.

The moving spot of fire grew rapidly, enlarged, took shape. It was a tiny stream of energy, like the tail of a tiny comet. It came still closer. Now they could see a flash of white and silver at its core, and still it drew closer. Now it took definite shape, a tiny body of metal and paint riding down on a long stream of atomic fire!

Then in mere seconds it hung over them, no longer tiny but a giant tower of polished metal hanging over the crater floor, falling ever more slowly, its great column of rocket fire reaching and scorching the surface of the rock. And suddenly, the fire was gone, there was a faint thud felt through the ground, and the two brothers stood staring.

Out there, not very distant, was standing a glorious, tall, slender rocket ship, fresh with paint, beautifully and delicately balanced on finely tapered fins, graceful as only a space craft can be.

On its side, clearly visible in the sunlight, was a large blue circle on which was superimposed the white star of the United States Air Force. There were numbers and things and a small, black air lock now opening near the nose of the rocket, but Robin and Peter hardly noticed these through the tears of joy that sprang to their eyes as they ran and bounded over the Moon's surface to greet their rescuers. Waving their hands, shouting, heedless of whether they were being heard, they were Robinson Crusoes no longer. They were on their way home.

THE END

If you've enjoyed this book, you will not want to miss these terrific titles…

ARMCHAIR SCI-FI & HORROR DOUBLE NOVELS, $12.95 each

D-1   **THE GALAXY RAIDERS** by William P. McGivern
           SPACE STATION #1 by Frank Belknap Long

D-2   **THE PROGRAMMED PEOPLE** by Jack Sharkey
           SLAVES OF THE CRYSTAL BRAIN by William Carter Sawtelle

D-3   **YOU'RE ALL ALONE** by Fritz Leiber
           THE LIQUID MAN by Bernard C. Gilford

D-4   **CITADEL OF THE STAR LORDS** by Edmond Hamilton
           VOYAGE TO ETERNITY by Milton Lesser

D-5   **IRON MEN OF VENUS** by Don Wilcox
           THE MAN WITH ABSOLUTE MOTION by Noel Loomis

D-6   **WHO SOWS THE WIND…** by Rog Phillips
           THE PUZZLE PLANET by Robert A. W. Lowndes

D-7   **PLANET OF DREAD** by Murray Leinster
           TWICE UPON A TIME by Charles L. Fontenay

D-8   **THE TERROR OUT OF SPACE** by Dwight V. Swain
           QUEST OF THE GOLDEN APE by Ivar Jorgensen and Adam Chase

D-9   **SECRET OF MARRACOTT DEEP** by Henry Slesar
           PAWN OF THE BLACK FLEET by Mark Clifton.

D-10   **BEYOND THE RINGS OF SATURN** by Robert Moore Williams
           A MAN OBSESSED by Alan E. Nourse

ARMCHAIR SCIENCE FICTION CLASSICS, $12.95 each

C-1   **THE GREEN MAN**
           by Harold M. Sherman

C-2   **A TRACE OF MEMORY**
           By Keith Laumer

C-3   **INTO PLUTONIAN DEPTHS**
           by Stanton A. Coblentz

ARMCHAIR MASTERS OF SCIENCE FICTION SERIES, $16.95 each

M-1   **MASTERS OF SCIENCE FICTION, Vol. One**
           Bryce Walton—"Dark of the Moon" and other tales

M-2   **MASTERS OF SCIENCE FICTION, Vol. Two**
           Jerome Bixby—"One Way Street" and other tales

If you've enjoyed this book, you will not want to miss these terrific titles…

ARMCHAIR SCI-FI & HORROR DOUBLE NOVELS, $12.95 each

D-11   **PERIL OF THE STARMEN** by Kris Neville
THE STRANGE INVASION by Murray Leinster

D-12   **THE STAR LORD** by Boyd Ellanby
CAPTIVES OF THE FLAME by Samuel R. Delany

D-13   **MEN OF THE MORNING STAR** by Edmond Hamilton
PLANET FOR PLUNDER by Hal Clement and Sam Merwin, Jr.

D-14   **ICE CITY OF THE GORGON** by Chester S. Geier and Richard Shaver
WHEN THE WORLD TOTTERED by Lester del Rey

D-15   **WORLDS WITHOUT END** by Clifford D. Simak
THE LAVENDER VINE OF DEATH by Don Wilcox

D-16   **SHADOW ON THE MOON** by Joe Gibson
ARMAGEDDON EARTH by Geoff St. Reynard

D-17   **THE GIRL WHO LOVED DEATH** by Paul W. Fairman
SLAVE PLANET by Laurence M. Janifer

D-18   **SECOND CHANCE** by J. F. Bone
MISSION TO A DISTANT STAR by Frank Belknap Long

D-19   **THE SYNDIC** by C. M. Kornbluth
FLIGHT TO FOREVER by Poul Anderson

D-20   **SOMEWHERE I'LL FIND YOU** by Milton Lesser
THE TIME ARMADA by Fox B. Holden

ARMCHAIR SCIENCE FICTION CLASSICS, $12.95 each

C-4   **CORPUS EARTHLING**
by Louis Charbonneau

C-5   **THE TIME DISSOLVER**
by Jerry Sohl

C-6   **WEST OF THE SUN**
by Edgar Pangborn

ARMCHAIR SCI-FI & HORROR GEMS SERIES, $12.95 each

G-1   **SCIENCE FICTION GEMS, Vol. One**
Isaac Asimov and others

G-2   **HORROR GEMS, Vol. One**
Carl Jacobi and others

If you've enjoyed this book, you will not want to miss these terrific titles...

ARMCHAIR SCI-FI & HORROR DOUBLE NOVELS, $12.95 each

D-21 **EMPIRE OF EVIL** by Robert Arnette
THE SIGN OF THE TIGER by Alan E. Nourse & J. A. Meyer

D-22 **OPERATION SQUARE PEG** by Frank Belknap Long
ENCHANTRESS OF VENUS by Leigh Brackett

D-23 **THE LIFE WATCH** by Lester del Rey
CREATURES OF THE ABYSS by Murray Leinster

D-24 **LEGION OF LAZARUS** by Edmond Hamilton
STAR HUNTER by Andre Norton

D-25 **EMPIRE OF WOMEN** by John Fletcher
ONE OF OUR CITIES IS MISSING by Irving Cox

D-26 **THE WRONG SIDE OF PARADISE** by Raymond F. Jones
THE INVOLUNTARY IMMORTALS by Rog Phillips

D-27 **EARTH QUARTER** by Damon Knight
ENVOY TO NEW WORLDS by Keith Laumer

D-28 **SLAVES TO THE METAL HORDE** by Milton Lesser
HUNTERS OUT OF TIME by Joseph E. Kelleam

D-29 **RX JUPITER SAVE US** by Ward Moore
BEWARE THE USURPERS by Geoff St. Reynard

D-30 **SECRET OF THE SERPENT** by Don Wilcox
CRUSADE ACROSS THE VOID by Dwight V. Swain

ARMCHAIR SCIENCE FICTION CLASSICS, $12.95 each

C-7 **THE SHAVER MYSTERY, Book One**
by Richard S. Shaver

C-8 **THE SHAVER MYSTERY, Book Two**
by Richard S. Shaver

C-9 **MURDER IN SPACE**
by David V. Reed

ARMCHAIR MASTERS OF SCIENCE FICTION SERIES, $16.95 each

M-3 **MASTERS OF SCIENCE FICTION, Vol. Three**
Robert Sheckley, "The Perfect Woman" and other tales

M-4 **MASTERS OF SCIENCE FICTION, Vol. Four**
Mack Reynolds, Part One, "Stowaway" and other tales

If you've enjoyed this book, you will not want to miss these terrific titles…

ARMCHAIR SCI-FI & HORROR DOUBLE NOVELS, $12.95 each

D-51 **A GOD NAMED SMITH** by Henry Slesar
        WORLDS OF THE IMPERIUM by Keith Laumer

D-52 **CRAIG'S BOOK** by Don Wilcox
        EDGE OF THE KNIFE by H. Beam Piper

D-53 **THE SHINING CITY** by Rena M. Vale
        THE RED PLANET by Russ Winterbotham

D-54 **THE MAN WHO LIVED TWICE** by Rog Phillips
        VALLEY OF THE CROEN by Lee Tarbell

D-55 **OPERATION DISASTER** by Milton Lesser
        LAND OF THE DAMNED by Berkeley Livingston

D-56 **CAPTIVE OF THE CENTAURIANESS** by Poul Anderson
        A PRINCESS OF MARS by Edgar Rice Burroughs

D-57 **THE NON-STATISTICAL MAN** by Raymond F. Jones
        MISSION FROM MARS by Rick Conroy

D-58 **INTRUDERS FROM THE STARS** by Ross Rocklynne
        FLIGHT OF THE STARLING by Chester S. Geier

D-59 **COSMIC SABOTEUR** by Frank M. Robinson
        LOOK TO THE STARS by Willard Hawkins

D-60 **THE MOON IS HELL!** by John W. Campbell, Jr.
        THE GREEN WORLD by Hal Clement

ARMCHAIR SCIENCE FICTION CLASSICS, $12.95 each

C-16 **THE SHAVER MYSTERY, Book Three**
        by Richard S. Shaver

C-17 **THE PLANET STRAPPERS**
        by Raymond Z. Gallun

C-18 **THE FOURTH "R"**
        by George O. Smith

ARMCHAIR SCI-FI & HORROR GEMS SERIES, $12.95 each

G-5 **SCIENCE FICTION GEMS, Vol. Three**
       C. M. Kornbluth and others

G-6 **HORROR GEMS, Vol. Three**
       August Derleth and others

If you've enjoyed this book, you will not want to miss these terrific titles...

ARMCHAIR SCI-FI & HORROR DOUBLE NOVELS, $12.95 each

ARMCHAIR SCIENCE FICTION CLASSICS, $12.95 each

ARMCHAIR SCI-FI & HORROR GEMS SERIES, $12.95 each

If you've enjoyed this book, you will not want to miss these terrific titles…

ARMCHAIR SCI-FI & HORROR DOUBLE NOVELS, $12.95 each

D-81 **THE LAST PLEA** by Robert Bloch
THE STATUS CIVILIZATION by Robert Sheckley

D-82 **WOMAN FROM ANOTHER PLANET** by Frank Belknap Long
HOMECALLING by Judith Merril

D-83 **WHEN TWO WORLDS MEET** by Robert Moore Williams
THE MAN WHO HAD NO BRAINS by Jeff Sutton

D-84 **THE SPECTRE OF SUICIDE SWAMP** by E. K. Jarvis
IT'S MAGIC, YOU DOPE! by Jack Sharkey

D-85 **THE STARSHIP FROM SIRIUS** by Rog Phillips
FINAL WEAPON by Everett Cole

D-86 **TREASURE ON THUNDER MOON** by Edmond Hamilton
TRAIL OF THE ASTROGAR by Henry Haase

D-87 **THE VENUS ENIGMA** by Joe Gibson
THE WOMAN IN SKIN 13 by Paul W. Fairman

D-88 **THE MAD ROBOT** by William P. McGivern
THE RUNNING MAN by J. Holly Hunter

D-89 **VENGEANCE OF KYVOR** by Randall Garrett
AT THE EARTH'S CORE by Edgar Rice Burroughs

D-90 **DWELLERS OF THE DEEP** by Don Wilcox
NIGHT OF THE LONG KNIVES by Fritz Leiber

ARMCHAIR SCIENCE FICTION CLASSICS, $12.95 each

C-28 **THE MAN FROM TOMORROW**
by Stanton A. Coblentz

C-29 **THE GREEN MAN OF GRAYPEC**
by Festus Pragnell

C-30 **THE SHAVER MYSTERY, Book Four**
by Richard S. Shaver

ARMCHAIR MASTERS OF SCIENCE FICTION SERIES, $16.95 each

MS-7 **MASTERS OF SCIENCE FICTION AND FANTASY, Vol. Seven**
Lester del Rey, "The Band Played On" and other tales

MS-8 **MASTERS OF SCIENCE FICTION, Vol. Eight**
Milton Lesser, "'A' as in Android" and other tales

If you've enjoyed this book, you will not want to miss these terrific titles...

ARMCHAIR SCI-FI & HORROR DOUBLE NOVELS, $12.95 each

ARMCHAIR SCIENCE FICTION CLASSICS, $12.95 each

ARMCHAIR SCI-FI & HORROR GEMS SERIES, $12.95 each